"Just exactly how old are you?"

Rhodri asked the question abruptly.

Hilary hesitated, then thought better of adding on a few years. "Twenty," she said reluctantly.

"Is that all?" Color flared unexpectedly along Rhodri's cheekbones for a moment. "I had no idea you were so young. Candida said you were qualified, and I assumed you were well into your twenties."

"I was rather a bright child," she informed him expressionlessly.

He smiled ruefully. "I think I'd better leave you to get on with your growing up, Hilary. You've more of it to do than I realized."

"Goodbye then," said Hilary slowly. "I'm sorry you came such a long way for nothing."

"Not entirely for nothing, Hilary," Rhodri said roughly, then bent swiftly and kissed her mouth with an abrupt force that was over before she could protest.

Catherine George was born in Wales, and
following her marriage to an engineer, lived eight
years in Brazil at a gold mine site. It was an
experience she would later draw upon for her
books, when she and her husband returned to
England. Now her husband helps manage their
household so that Catherine can devote more time
to her writing. They have two children, a daughter
and a son, who share their mother's love of
language and writing.

Books by Catherine George

HARLEQUIN ROMANCE

2535—RELUCTANT PARAGON
2571—DREAM OF MIDSUMMER
2720—DESIRABLE PROPERTY
2822—THE FOLLY OF LOVING
2924—MAN OF IRON
2942—THIS TIME ROUND

HARLEQUIN PRESENTS

1016—LOVE LIES SLEEPING
1065—TOUCH ME IN THE MORNING
1152—VILLAIN OF THE PIECE
1184—TRUE PARADISE
1225—LOVEKNOT
1255—EVER SINCE EDEN

CONSOLATION PRIZE

Catherine George

Harlequin Books

TORONTO • NEW YORK • LONDON
AMSTERDAM • PARIS • SYDNEY • HAMBURG
STOCKHOLM • ATHENS • TOKYO • MILAN

Original hardcover edition published in 1989
by Mills & Boon Limited

ISBN 0-373-03081-9

Harlequin Romance first edition October 1990

CHAPTER ONE

THE instructions on the jar of face pack were simple. A layer of the contents smoothed on, a wait of ten minutes, and presto—a glowing, radiant skin. Hilary swathed a towel turban-wise over her wet hair, wrapped herself in her sister's white towelling bathrobe and rubbed a place clear on the bathroom mirror to inspect her face. Even through a cloud of steam it was perfectly plain that her skin neither glowed nor radiated, even after a hot bath. She sighed, then reached for the jar. Her sister Candida's skin never failed to glow, so if the face pack was in any way responsible it seemed silly not to try some herself.

The green cream smelt of cucumber and mint, and felt ice-cold on Hilary's warm skin. She smeared on a thick layer, then surveyed the result in the mirror. Choking back a snort of laughter, because the instructions forbade any facial movement while the green goo did its stuff, she went into the bedroom to relax as advised.

She stretched herself on the bed, apprehensive as the cream on her face hardened in seconds to what felt like baked mud. It tugged at her skin and gave off fumes which made her eyes stream as the cucumber and mint gave way to something rather more reminiscent of the chemistry lab in school. After a minute or two of wondering if it was all worth it, Hilary suddenly sat bolt upright as she heard sounds from downstairs. Her heart thumped. Candida wasn't due home for hours, and Nell, who shared the house, had gone out ages ago.

Since a scream was not only useless but a physical impossibility, Hilary edged stealthily off the bed and peered about her for something to use in self-defence. To her surprise she found Candida's old hockey-stick on the floor near the bed and seized on it thankfully, then turned the knob as quietly as she could on the bedroom door and crept out on the landing.

Fighting an overpowering desire to sniff as tears from the sulphurous fumes almost blinded her, she crouched down and peered myopically through the banisters, her blood running cold as her worst fears were confirmed. The sitting-room door was wide open, and there, bending over the video in the corner, was a dark, frightening male shape. Hilary launched instinctively into action, hurling herself down the stairs, hockey-stick at the ready.

The man sprang to his feet as she burst into the room but, without giving herself time to think better of it, Hilary leapt in the air and brought her weapon crashing down on the intruder's head. He went down like a felled tree, to the accompaniment of loud screams from the doorway and the crash of crockery as Candida Mason dropped a tray of coffee-mugs and flew across the room to kneel by the fallen intruder. She was followed closely by a tall, dark man who looked vaguely familiar to the shattered Hilary.

'Oh, heavens!' Candida wailed, and patted the unconscious man's hand feverishly. 'Are you all right?' Since it was quite obvious he was anything but all right, Candida turned on her shrinking sister like a tigress. 'What in heaven's name did you do *that* for, you little idiot? You've half-killed him, by the look of it.'

'I thought he was a burglar,' mumbled Hilary, through mud-stiff lips.

Candida groaned, then turned back to the sufferer, who was showing signs of life. He moaned, and, weak with relief, Hilary flew to ease a cushion under his blond head as Candida held it gently supported.

'What happened?' a musical voice said groggily. 'Who——?' Grey eyes opened on Hilary's face, widened in horror and shut tightly again, a shudder running through his body. The man bending over him chuckled.

'Don't worry, Rod. I won't let her hit you again.'

'Jack!' Candida scowled at him, and turned to Hilary's victim. 'It's all right,' she assured him. 'You're not having a nightmare. That's my sister.'

'Why is she green?' asked the invalid faintly, apparently afraid to open his eyes again.

'Face pack,' mumbled Hilary indistinctly. 'Should I call a doctor?'

Gingerly, with help from Candida and the highly amused Jack, the man sat up, and eyed Hilary askance, wincing as he touched a hand to his temple, where blood trickled from a small cut. 'Not unless you need surgery to remove that stuff!'

Angry colour flared unseen in Hilary's cheeks. 'I thought *you* might need medical attention, Mr——'

Candida gave her sister an exasperated frown. 'Do go and wash that stuff off, Hilly, you look an absolute fright!'

'Very true,' said the injured man with feeling. 'She scared the living daylights out of me.'

Candida gave him an embarrassed smile, recollecting herself hurriedly. 'This is my sister Hilary, of course. Hilly, this is Rhodri Lloyd-Ellis.'

'How about me?' said the other man, sounding injured. He relieved Hilary of the hockey-stick with a brilliant smile on his spectacularly handsome face, and shook her reluctant hand. 'I'm Rhodri's cousin, John Wynne Jones.'

'Oh, no,' choked Hilary through mud-stiff lips, wishing the floor would open up and swallow her.

'Oh, yes!' said Candida grimly. 'Off you go.'

Hilary beat a hasty retreat, burningly conscious of two pairs of amused male eyes watching her scuttle up the stairs, one pair black and brilliant, in a face known to fans of both theatre and television, and the other a piercingly clear grey, with laughter-lines raying from the corners.

In an agony of embarrassment and remorse Hilary flew up to the bathroom to splash water on her face as instructed on the jar of face pack. How unkind fate could be sometimes! So that was John Wynne Jones in the spectacular flesh, she thought in despair, as she splashed and hacked away at the green mud, which had now hardened to the consistency of plaster of Paris. Candida had met him at the wedding of a schoolfriend in the summer, and had never stopped talking about him since. Which was perfectly understandable, since he was an actor of growing repute, and quite the best-looking man Hilary had ever seen in her life. Bar one. She swallowed hard at the thought of the man she'd assaulted, shuddering at the way she'd borne down on him like something out of a horror film and knocked him cold. Jack Wynne Jones deserved his description as one of the best-looking actors in the profession, she conceded, but as far as she was concerned his cousin had him beaten into a cocked hat for looks. Hilary winced at the word 'beaten', and gave a despairing sigh. A good thing she was off to her new job in a few days' time. Candida was likely to be very unforgiving towards her little sister, and rightly so, for making such a ghastly scene in front of the gorgeous Jack she'd talked about so much.

It took some time to get rid of the face pack. And when all traces of it had, not without difficulty, been finally removed, the results bore no resemblance at all to the glow and radiance promised on the jar. Hilary viewed her face with alarm. It glowed beet-red, and went on doing so, even after several applications of Candida's Soothing Honey Lotion. Her hair was almost as bad. Forgotten in the press of recent events, it had dried under its towel to a wild, wiry mop which refused to lie down however much she attacked it with a hairbrush.

When her frantic efforts to subdue it only served to intensify the raw, angry colour of her face, Hilary gave up in despair and pulled on jersey and jeans, shivering a little now the excitement was over. She wished miserably she could just crawl into bed and pull the covers over her head, but knew that just wasn't on. She had no alternative but to go back downstairs and face the music. She procrastinated for a while, trying to compose graceful phrases of apology to deliver to the fair, handsome man with the Welsh name she couldn't even remember, then winced as Candida called up to her, in a voice that meant business.

'Hilary! Could you come down here, please?'

Hilary blew out her raw, scarlet cheeks and went downstairs on leaden feet.

Candida had cleared away the debris of broken china, and was dispensing coffee to her two visitors. To Hilary's relief, apart from a plaster on his forehead and a slight pallor, her victim looked reassuringly little the worse for wear.

'Come on in, Hilary,' said Candida, and smiled affectionately. 'It's all right, love. No one's going to bite you.'

Hilary felt it was hardly the occasion to resent the indulgence in her sister's voice, and thanked her lucky stars Candida sounded friendly again. Her sister was normally as good-natured as she was beautiful, and it had been quite harrowing earlier to be the object of her rare censure. Hilary smiled back at Candida despairingly, then turned to the men who had risen to their feet as she appeared. Jack Wynne Jones's face was wreathed in smiles, but his fair, elegant cousin, who looked dauntingly sophisticated and mature now that Hilary had time to look at him properly, was studying her in a frankly dissecting fashion which made her hackles rise.

'Please accept my apologies, Mr——' began Hilary stiffly, then coloured even more as she racked her brain to remember his name.

'Lloyd-Ellis,' he said helpfully, with a smile which lit up his face to such a degree that it stopped Hilary in her tracks. 'But since our introduction was, you'll admit, distinctly unorthodox, I think first names are in order, don't you?'

Hilary pulled herself together with an effort and made her answering smile cool. 'If you like—Lloyd.'

'No, no, *cariad*,' interrupted Jack, patting a place beside him on the sofa. 'His name's Rhodri. The rest of it is his surname. We Welsh are a bit greedy about names, we often like two or three. Mind you,' he added, grinning, 'so many of us have the same surname that if we didn't tack another one on to it we'd never know who was who.'

Hilary gave him a warm smile, grateful to the irrepressible actor for putting her at her ease. 'I see what you mean. I suppose plain ''John Jones'' could have been a disadvantage for you as an actor.'

Candida's sea-blue eyes held an unusually cynical gleam as they rested on Jack's face. 'I don't know I agree with you there, Hilly.'

'Oh?' said Jack quickly, the smile suddenly absent. 'Why?'

Candida smiled serenely. '"A rose by any other name" and all that. You're the Shakespeare wallah, so you know what I mean.'

'She means you're so pretty, Jack,' said Rhodri drily, 'that it wouldn't matter whether your name was John Wynne Jones or Joe Bloggs, people would still pay to see you perform.'

Hilary watched, riveted, as Jack looked distinctly put out at the thought. He turned to her almost as if embarrassed, plunging into a discussion on her own taste in films.

Hilary would have liked nothing better than to indulge in idle chitchat with a man she was more used to seeing on a cinema screen than alongside her on her sister's sofa, but, mindful that Jack was the man Candida had been talking about non-stop every time Hilary had been in her company lately, she decided it best after only a few minutes to return to the apology she'd been in the middle of making to his cousin.

'I apologise for hitting you like that—Rhodri,' she said doggedly. 'I honestly thought you were a burglar, and as I'm just a visitor here I felt responsible. I was sure you were making off with Candida's video, you see, so I had to stop you somehow.'

'And you did!' said Rhodri Lloyd-Ellis with feeling. 'Not that I had any designs on the video. I was about to record some programme for your sister, while she was making coffee in the kitchen with Jack, then suddenly I was set upon by a pint-sized fury, complete with turban and green face.'

Hilary's colour, which had begun to subside, surged back again as the grey, crystalline eyes danced at her expense.

'Here, Hilary, have some coffee,' said Candida, aware of her sister's distress. 'And for heaven's sake don't use that stuff again. It must be years old, for a start—it might damage your skin.'

'I think it already has. Whereas my aim was to encourage it to look more like yours,' said Hilary, sighing.

'There's nothing wrong with your skin,' said Candida firmly.

'Nor your right arm, either,' added Rhodri, grinning. 'You wield a mean hockey-stick young lady. Were you star of the school team?'

'No.' Hilary gave a mischievous look in her sister's direction. 'Candida was, though. It's her hockey-stick.'

Jack turned wicked black eyes on Candida's flushed face in exaggerated surprise. 'I wouldn't have taken you for a sporting type, Candida, somehow.'

'Why should you?' said Candida, in a tart voice Hilary was sure she never employed with any male as a rule. 'Our acquaintance is, after all, very slight.'

Jack smiled very slowly, his eyes assessing, Hilary saw, as though his interest in her sister had suddenly intensified. 'That could be remedied. Couldn't it?'

Candida made no reply, her eyes on Rhodri's face, which had taken on a very unhealthy-looking pallor.

'Are you all right, Rhodri?' she demanded.

Hilary felt thoroughly depressed. Just her luck, she thought miserably, to get off on the wrong foot with such an attractive man. She took herself in hand, swiftly. What was she thinking about? The man was probably married, and in any case it was highly unlikely he'd ever have given her a second glance with Candida in the immediate vicinity. She bit her lip. Of course, no one could say Hilary Mason hadn't *made* an impression on the urbane, double-barrelled Mr Lloyd-Ellis. Unfortunately it was entirely the wrong kind.

'A bit of a headache,' confessed her victim, and smiled reassuringly at his stricken assailant. 'But nothing a couple of aspirins and a good night's sleep won't put right.' He got to his feet and swayed a little.

'A good thing Jack's driving you home,' said Candida, looking worried.

'I'm not sure I agree,' he said lightly. 'A trip home in that flash car of Jack's will probably give me a relapse.'

Jack looked injured. 'Rubbish. Anyway, since I'm the only chauffeur you've got, friend, let's be on our way— I'll drive very sedately all the way to your place, I promise.'

Despite the badinage he exchanged with his cousin, Hilary had a strong suspicion that Rhodri Lloyd-Ellis was feeling pretty seedy as she went with her sister to see the men off, since he leaned on Jack's arm for the last few steps, pretending extreme frailty to cover the fact that he wasn't very steady on his feet.

'Take more water with it next time, old son,' said Jack cheerfully, but Hilary could see he took care as he settled his cousin in the passenger seat of the low-slung sports car standing at the kerb.

'I hope you'll be all right,' said Candida, leaning down to the open car window to peer anxiously at Rhodri's pale face.

'Don't worry,' he said lightly. 'I've got a thick skull— hopefully.' He looked beyond Candida to where Hilary stood silent in the darkness at the gate. 'Goodnight, Hilary,' he said, in a depressingly avuncular tone.

'Goodnight,' she answered quietly. 'I'm terribly sorry I hurt you.'

'Think nothing of it,' he said promptly, and smiled up at Candida. 'A crack on the head is a small price to pay for making the acquaintance of two lovely ladies.'

'Right,' said Jack, sounding irritable. 'If you've finished with the fond farewells, we'll get going. Goodnight, ladies. I'll give you a ring tomorrow, Candida.'

'Fine,' she answered casually. 'Goodnight.'

Jack turned the key in the ignition, but instead of the roar Hilary expected from the engine the car gave a few asthmatic wheezes, then fell silent. Its owner cursed, then tried again, coaxing and wheedling, even threatening his beloved car, but to no avail.

'I don't know why you don't buy a decent car,' remarked Rhodri, grinning through the open window at the watching girls as Jack cursed sibilantly in Welsh.

'Don't insult her or she'll never start!' he said in despair.

'She isn't going to start anyway, is she?' said Rhodri. 'Perhaps Candida would ring for a taxi instead.'

'Oh, you don't need to do that,' said Candida promptly, and waved a hand towards the red Mini parked a few feet away. 'Hilary will run you home in *her* car. I don't drive, I'm afraid,' she added, giving Hilary a secret dig in the ribs.

Hilary picked up her cue, trying to sound enthusiastic. 'Yes, of course. No trouble. I'll run in and get my keys.' She hurried inside, wondering what she'd done to deserve all this as she dashed upstairs and collected her car keys. A hurried glance in the hall mirror as she ran down again confirmed that her face, while not quite so scarlet, had a raw, sore look about it that made her feel as attractive as a boiled lobster.

Grateful for the darkness outside, she unlocked her little car quickly and suggested Jack get in the back before Candida gave her a hand to help the now frankly wavering Rhodri into the passenger seat.

'Sorry—to—be such a nuisance,' he panted, as Candida stood back so that Hilary could secure the seatbelt.

'*I* was the nuisance,' said Hilary ruefully, and slid behind the wheel as Jack leaned forward to wave to Candida as the car moved off.

Hilary asked for directions, wishing fervently that Candida *had* learnt to drive as she headed along unfamiliar roads to the house where Rhodri Lloyd-Ellis lived, on the outskirts of Oxford. It was a lowering experience to feel certain that both men in the car, however friendly and polite they were to their young chauffeur, would have preferred her place taken by her beautiful sister. To be fair, neither man's manners allowed him to be obvious about it. Nevertheless, Hilary was deeply thankful when they arrived in a quiet, tree-lined road, where Rhodri told her to park outside an attractive, solid-looking house standing just inside a pair of tall iron gates. Once they were out of the car, she comforted herself, she would make her getaway. Fast.

She jumped out of the car and went round to help Rhodri, not without some difficulty, and in the end Jack slithered out via the driver's seat and tore round to help, as Hilary tried to get her shoulder under Rhodri's arm to keep him upright.

'Sorry,' said Rhodri regretfully. 'My legs seem to be made of spaghetti.'

'Right-o, then, Rod,' said Jack, and draped his cousin's arm round his shoulders. 'Could you take his other arm, *cariad*? He's waving about a bit.'

Hilary groaned silently, and thrust her arm through Rhodri's, unhappily aware of his body's proximity through the dark city suit as she lent her support through the iron gates.

'Where are your keys, Rod?' asked Jack as they arrived at the double doors of the house.

'Trouser pocket, right-hand side,' muttered Rhodri, sounding strained.

'Your side, Hilary,' said Jack. 'Fish 'em out, there's a good girl.'

How old did they think she was? she thought crossly, as, with great reluctance, she slid a hand into the pocket indicated, feeling horribly flustered as she came into contact with a fair amount of thinly-covered muscular thigh in the process, before she located the pair of keys in question.

Hilary unlocked the heavy oak doors, then another pair of doors made of stained glass with an air of William Morris about it, and a few moments later Rhodri was deposited on an oak settle in a square hall floored with black and white tiles which gave a cool, Dutch impression.

'You look very pale,' she said anxiously, as she bent over the slumped man, then jumped back as he gave her a wicked glance very much at variance with the white line of strain about his beautifully-shaped mouth.

'Which is more than can be said for *you*, Hilary.'

She glared at him, and Jack intervened swiftly. 'Come on, Rod, we'd better get you to bed.'

We? Hilary eyed him with suspicion. 'Can't you manage on your own now?'

Jack smiled encouragingly. 'Probably, love, but I'd be a lot happier if you'd just give me a hand with him up those stairs.' He gave her a look even more wicked than his cousin's. 'Don't worry, though, I expect I'll manage to undress him all by myself.'

'She's too small,' said Rhodri suddenly. 'She'll hurt herself. I can manage.' He pushed himself to his feet, then swayed slightly and the other two made a grab for him.

'I'm sure I'll survive a trip up the stairs,' Hilary assured him, resigned, and cast a peremptory blue eye at Jack. 'But could we get it over, please, so he can get to bed where he belongs?'

'Pity your sister couldn't have come instead,' panted Rhodri, as they manhandled him up the staircase which, to Hilary's relief, was wide enough to make their progress at least relatively easy.

'Amen to that,' said Hilary, so bitterly that Jack scowled at his cousin.

'Don't be so bloody ungrateful, Rod!'

'I meant,' gasped Rhodri, looking more ghastly by the minute, 'that Candida might be more willowy than our cuddly young Hilary here, but she is at least six inches taller, at a rough guess, which would make things easier.'

Not to mention the fact that you probably fancy my sister just as much as your cousin does, thought Hilary blackly, and would much prefer to have *her* pushing you up these beastly stairs than me.

When they finally reached the landing Hilary relinquished the invalid into Jack's care with a sigh of relief.

'There,' she said firmly. 'I'm sure you can manage now. I'll take myself off.'

'Hang on,' said Jack. 'Wait downstairs a minute, Hilary. I'll come down as soon as I've put Rod to bed.'

'Bathroom!' interrupted Rhodri with sudden violence, and Hilary retreated downstairs in a hurry, as Jack hauled his tall cousin through the nearest open door. Even from her seat on the oak settle in the hall below Hilary could hear sounds that indicated Rhodri was losing his dinner. It seemed a long time before he was settled in his bed afterwards. She had grown tired of examining the pattern on the thin, fringed rug on the floor by the time Jack came running down the stairs.

'Right, I've got him tucked up safe and sound,' he said, smiling at her warmly. 'Thank you, Hilary. You were a great help.'

'The least I could do since I caused all the trouble,' she said glumly. 'Are you sure your cousin doesn't need a doctor?'

'Quite sure. Says he feels tons better after being sick— and apologises for wearing you out, by the way,' added Jack with a twinkle.

'Nonsense,' said Hilary gruffly. 'Right, I'd best be off, then, or Candida will be worried.'

'Rod said I was to give you a drink, or coffee, or something, before you drive back——' began Jack, but Hilary shook her head firmly.

'No, thanks, I really must go. I hope your cousin feels better in the morning.'

'He will,' Jack assured her. 'Very fit chap, our Rod. Plays squash and frequents a gym too often to worry about a crack on the head from a little thing like you.'

Hilary was embarrassed rather than worried, furious with herself about the entire episode, one way and another. She made her goodbyes in a hurry, promising to tell Candida that Jack would be round next day to pick up his car.

'Well?' demanded Candida, pulling Hilary inside the house the moment she arrived back.

Hilary gave a brief description of the struggle to get Rhodri Lloyd-Ellis home and dry, and flopped down on a stool in the kitchen, looking morose as her sister made coffee.

'You're very quiet,' commented Candida.

'Mm,' agreed Hilary glumly.

'It was quite an evening, wasn't it?'

'Certainly was.'

'Don't be too embarrassed, love.'

'Wouldn't *you* be?'

'The question doesn't arise, Hilly, because *I* would never have been brave enough to attack an intruder!'

'Silly enough, you mean.' Hilary sighed deeply. 'It's time I learnt to be less impulsive.'

Candida patted her arm comfortingly as they went upstairs. 'It's an ill wind, love. Rhodri Lloyd-Ellis is a very attractive man, and he's hardly likely to forget meeting you, is he, under the circumstances?'

'I'd rather he did, believe me!'

'Don't you like him?'

'Yes,' said Hilary shortly. 'Not that it matters much. I don't pretend to be a raving beauty, but I have looked rather better on other occasions than I do tonight, you'll admit. Added to which, I'm sure he thinks I'm still in school! Courtesy of that blasted hockey-stick, I suppose, not to mention the scatty behaviour.'

'He was charming afterwards, love.'

'That was because of you. He hardly took his eyes off you once he could get them open again.'

'Rubbish!' said Candida astringently. 'Did you like Jack, by the way?'

Hilary's eyes narrowed. 'Yes. I did, actually. Why?'

'No reason.'

'Oh, come on,' teased Hilary. 'He's everything you said he was, *and* he's fun and not the least bit conceited either, which is pretty incredible with a face and body like his. Which reminds me,' she added. 'In all the fuss I never managed to find out just what John Wynne Jones was actually doing here, Candida, not to mention his unfortunate cousin.'

'Davina Lennox sent him—Davina Seymour now, of course.'

'*Sent* him?'

Candida nodded, looking rather wistful. 'She gave him my address and told him to look me up. So he did. Or was about to. In actual fact I was at the station, helping my boss and his brood off on their skiing trip after we finished his list tonight. His wife barely gave him time to draw breath after his last appointment before two taxis arrived to take them off on the first stage of their flight to La Plagne. I offered to lend a hand with all the bits and pieces, and was just about to come home in the taxi when Jack came dashing up. He was picking Rhodri up from the London train, and said he'd intended telephoning me later, so I invited them both home for a drink. I thought you'd enjoy meeting them.'

'Instead of which, of course, I caused absolute mayhem,' said Hilary with a despairing groan.

Candida didn't even hear. She had a faraway look in her blue eyes. 'It was a wonderful surprise seeing Jack just appear out of the blue like that. I hadn't seen him since Davy's wedding.'

'Of course—he was best man, wasn't he?'

Candida's smile was wry. 'Yes. The snag, of course, unless I'm much mistaken, is that it wasn't the role he would have cast himself in.'

'You don't mean——?'

'Oh, yes. Jack would have preferred a production with Davy as the bride, right enough, but with himself as bridegroom, not his pal Leo Seymour.'

Hilary forgot the embarrassment and excitement of the evening as she saw the shadow on her sister's face. 'And you think he's still carrying the same torch?' she said gently.

Candida nodded. 'Funny, really, isn't it? No one could ever say I've been short of male attention—but until now I've never cared two hoots about any of it.'

'You mean it goes that deep with Jack?' asked Hilary with concern.

'Yes, love. And he just happens to be in love with my best friend. Hilarious, isn't it?'

Hilary shook her head. She didn't consider it funny at all. She knew exactly how Candida felt—none better. Before tonight, admittedly, she would have found it hard to understand how any woman could make a fool of herself over a man. But one look at Rhodri Lloyd-Ellis had been all it took to discover how desperately easy it was, after all. While he, of course, naturally had only needed Candida in the offing to forget any other female even existed.

'Never mind,' said Candida, brightening. 'I've got something to be pleased about.' She beamed at Hilary. 'Jack's actually invited me to the premiére of his new film—the one he stars in as Byron.'

'You mean actually *go* to it with him?' said Hilary, impressed.

'Yes.' Candida's arresting blue eyes gleamed. 'Which is a very good beginning, wouldn't you say?'

Hilary assured her sister it was a brilliant beginning, and eventually went off to bed to lick her wounds in private, feeling emotionally battered. It was a long time before she could manage to laugh at herself, at the thought that Rhodri Lloyd-Ellis was likely to be feeling far worse, poor man. Her smile lingered as she thought of John Wynne Jones. A good thing, perhaps, that he was unaware of the plans Candida had for catching him on the rebound. Of the actor's handsome cousin Hilary flatly refused to think any more, apart from a strengthening reminder that the day after tomorrow she would be leaving Oxford behind for her new job, and would soon forget she'd ever met the man. It was unlikely that her pathetic little crush would survive unnourished by future sightings of its object.

So she experienced utter dismay when Candida came running into the cramped little spare-room the following morning, her eyes glittering with excitement.

Hilary heaved herself up in bed, eyeing her sister groggily. 'What's up? Shouldn't you be in work?'

'It's Saturday, muggins!' Candida gave a little war-dance. 'Guess what!'

Hilary, never at her best in the morning, refused to play guessing games. 'Just tell me what switched on your ignition, and go away and let me come to in my own good time.'

'All right then, Grumpy! I've just had a phone-call from Jack.'

'Congratulations,' said Hilary, and lay down again, pulling up the covers, only to have them snatched away again.

'Don't be such a misery!' scolded Candida, and sat down on the bed. 'First, in answer to the question you haven't yet had the grace to ask, you unfeeling creature, Rhodri is perfectly all right this morning.'

Hilary flushed with guilt. 'Sorry—I'm not really awake yet! Nevertheless, I'm glad I haven't injured him for life.'

'Then,' went on her sister, 'Jack said he was sending someone from a garage to pick up his car.'

'He's not coming himself, then.'

'Ah, but here comes the best part,' said Candida in triumph. 'He asked if by any miracle you and I were free to go out to dinner tonight.'

Hilary groaned. 'I sincerely hope you told him you were and I wasn't! I absolutely refuse to play goose-berry, Candida.'

'You don't have to. Cousin Rhodri's making up the four!'

CHAPTER TWO

ARGUMENTS, pleas, cajolery—nothing was any use. Candida was adamant. No way was Hilary going to wriggle out of the evening.

'Nonsense! Honestly, Hilary, you're the end. Any other girl would jump at the chance of a night out with a couple of escorts like Jack and his cousin.'

'Then *ask* some other girl! Perhaps Nell——'

'Nell is on night-shift at the hospital,' said Candida sternly.

'You must know someone else!'

'I do. But *you* were the one invited, Hilary Mason, so you're going whether you like it or not. Come on. Let's wash your hair. I'll perform a spot of magic on it afterwards with my trusty hair-drier.'

Hilary submitted to her sister's ministrations, thinking bitterly that it would take a great deal of magic to transform her own ash-brown mop into anything remotely like her sister's gleaming blonde glory. The only thing she had in common with Candida were the dark blue eyes inherited from their mother. Otherwise she had her father's wiry brown hair, olive skin, sturdy build, but unhappily not his height. At that point her mother's genes had stepped in again and decreed she grow no more than an inch or so over five feet, a good six inches shorter than the graceful Candida.

'Besides,' said Candida, as she wielded a brush expertly, 'a dinner at the Randolph isn't to be sneezed at.'

Hilary would have sold her soul for beans on toast at home, rather than watch Rhodri Lloyd-Ellis vie with his cousin for Candida's attention all night. It had been depressingly obvious that his meeting with Candida had affected him in exactly the same way as the rest of his sex, and tonight, dressed for the occasion, Candida's impact was likely to be even greater.

'I haven't anything very grand to wear,' Hilary warned.

'No matter.' Candida smiled cheerfully at her sister's glum face in the mirror. 'You can borrow something of mine.'

'No, thanks. Your stuff is too long—and too tight— for me. If I must go I'll wear the brown crêpe de Chine skirt I splashed out on yesterday with the money Mother gave me for Christmas.'

Candida frowned. 'You should have bought the black one.'

Hilary shook her head. 'I look hideous in black— makes my skin look sallow. Anyway, I can wear that gold sweater you made for me. Neat but not gaudy, and what's more I'll be warm. It's freezing out there.'

Candida was full of approval when they were finally ready to go. Hilary knew her appearance was the best she was ever likely to achieve, particularly since her hair looked much better than usual after Candida's ministrations, even consenting to wave rather than curl tightly about her face. To her relief her complexion had reverted to its usual even olive tint, and with the addition of her gold locket and chain, and the height lent by her best pair of shoes, Hilary felt slightly better about the evening ahead. Candida, ravishing in a wool dress the colour of her eyes, insisted that Hilary drink a glass of wine while they waited for the men to arrive.

'It'll do you good, Hilly. Put you in the mood.'

Hilary doubted that one glass of wine was anything like enough to do that, but obediently downed it, feeling warmer for it, if nothing else. She grinned at her sister. 'How about another? This one didn't reach my cold feet.'

'Not on an empty stomach, love.' Candida sprang to her feet at the sound of the doorbell, and went to let in Jack Wynne Jones. He looked utterly magnificent in a dark suit with a pearl-grey brocade waistcoat.

'Good evening, ladies,' he said with a flourishing bow. 'Your carriage awaits. Only it's a taxi with the meter running, so I respectfully suggest we get a move on.'

Hilary brightened as they were rushed from the house. Perhaps his elegant cousin wasn't coming, after all. Her hopes were quickly dashed as Jack slid between the two girls on the back seat of the taxi.

'Rod's meeting us there,' he informed them. 'Had to see a business contact first, so he'll be along later.'

Pity, thought Hilary. If she had to play the spare-wheel role she was used to in Candida's company, it would have been a lot better with only the ebullient Jack, who very quickly put her at ease by teasing her about her transformation from the night before.

'You look terrific tonight,' he said, after he'd paid off the taxi. He offered an arm to each girl as they went up the steps of the Randolph Hotel. 'Both of you,' he added, as he ushered them into the bar. 'But the difference in Hilary tonight is pretty remarkable, while you, Candida, always seem to look the same.'

'I've had more graceful compliments.' Candida's smile was rueful as Jack went off to the bar.

'*I* haven't,' said Hilary, and settled herself at the small table next to her sister, her back turned to the door. Perhaps if she willed it strongly enough Rhodri Lloyd-Ellis wouldn't turn up at all.

She was doomed to disappointment. The moment Jack returned with the drinks his cousin joined them, apologising for his tardiness with a charm Hilary viewed with misgiving. Last night, even battered and colourless after her stupid attack, Rhodri Lloyd-Ellis had made her heart flip over in her chest. Tonight he was something else entirely. His chalk-striped suit was less flamboyant than Jack's, but with his handsome face alight with greeting he was more than a match in looks for his famous cousin, and Hilary sternly quelled the pulse which leapt at the mere sight of him.

'It was very good of you to come tonight at such short notice,' he said, as he sat down between the two girls. His smile was directed at both of them with graceful impartiality, but Hilary, quite sure his remark was really meant for Candida, smiled up at Jack Wynne Jones with more than her customary warmth as he returned with a whisky and soda for his cousin.

'I'd kept tonight free, anyway,' said Candida, 'because it's Hilary's last evening in Oxford. She starts a new job next week. My clever little sister, despite her youth, is a B.Lib.'

Not overjoyed to find herself thrust into the spotlight, Hilary explained that she was about to begin her first post as a librarian, and was looking forward to it, because it was rural and would involve a regular stint with the mobile library which served the area.

'You watch out for amorous farmers, then,' said Jack, laughing. 'Don't let them corner you in your van.'

'I imagine I'm more likely to meet their wives. I thought farmers worked so hard and so long they never had time to read!'

'And having no time to read is Hilary's personal idea of purgatory, of course,' said Candida indulgently. 'That's why she didn't hear me call when we got in last night. She was reading in the bath.'

Hilary flushed, and applied herself to her drink, wishing Candida had kept quiet about the disastrous events of the evening before.

Rhodri, plainly aware of her embarrassment, smiled at her warmly. 'In which case I imagine you can give your clients synopses of your entire stock, then, Miss Mason?'

'Oh, first names, please!' said Candida, and gave him the benefit of her dazzling smile.

She caught Hilary's eye meaningfully, but Hilary ignored her sister's discreet little dart of disapproval. It was utterly beyond her to respond to Rhodri's friendly overtures because nothing could convince her that they weren't prompted by mere good manners; that his real preference was to devote himself to Candida. Hilary applied herself to Jack Wynne Jones instead, finding him very easy to talk to as she asked eager questions about the films he'd recently made, and the play he was currently rehearsing. Half-way through her second gin and tonic Hilary realised the drinks were doubles, very conscious of the fact as a waiter ushered them to a table at one of the long windows looking out on Beaumont Street. Her knees felt alarmingly wobbly, and she was glad to sit down in the chair Rhodri Lloyd-Ellis held out for her. To her surprise he seated himself alongside her, leaving Jack to sit opposite with Candida.

A pianist was playing sophisticated background music as the four of them went through the little ceremony of choosing the wine. The strains of Gershwin and Kern provided a slight screen of privacy over their conversation as Rhodri turned to Hilary afterwards and said quietly, 'I'm afraid you're still suffering from embarrassment after last night, Hilary. If I may call you Hilary?'

'I thought first names were decided on some time ago.' She busied herself with flicking out the large starched napkin.

'By your sister, not you.' He shrugged ruefully. 'If you prefer I'll stick to "Miss Mason".'

Hilary turned frosty blue eyes on him. 'It really doesn't matter. Our acquaintance is unlikely to be more than fleeting.'

His eyes darkened. 'I rather fancy I've committed some crime far worse than falling victim to your hockey-stick. Won't you enlighten me?'

Tell him she'd resented being treated like a backward child? No way, thought Hilary. 'The crime was all mine, of course,' she said lightly. 'I wouldn't have blamed you in the slightest if you'd been furious with me, rather than so sporting about it.'

'I was flabbergasted rather than furious.' He gave her a narrowed, sidelong glance. 'I'll admit I thought—when I was *able* to think again—that you were very much younger than you are. You look amazingly different tonight.'

'Isn't that the truth!' chimed in Jack with a wicked grin, as he overheard the last. 'When Hilary assaulted you with her trusty hockey-stick I bet it wasn't the thwack which knocked you cold—more likely naked fear at the mere sight of her with her white draperies and green face!'

Candida gave him a scorching look as Hilary's cheeks flushed bright scarlet with embarrassment. 'Do shut up, Jack!' She smiled across at Rhodri. 'You know what weird things we women do to ourselves, Rhodri. We just happened to interrupt Hilly in the middle of a home beauty treatment.'

'And in all the fuss I left the stuff on too long—which was why I looked like a rising sun later on,' said Hilary, trying to ignore her blazing cheeks.

'And is it still working?' inquired Rhodri silkily. 'Or is your present colour due to my cousin's lamentable manners?'

'Sorry, *cariad*,' said Jack, and smiled penitently. 'Don't mind me—famous for my lack of tact.'

To Hilary's relief their first course arrived at that point, and in the ensuing little bustle of activity the subject was dropped. Less embarrassing topics of conversation were maintained for the rest of dinner. Even so none of the dishes served to her made much impression on her taste-buds. She could see that Rhodri noticed her lack of appetite, and blessed the good manners which prevented him from commenting on it, but she only began to feel relatively at ease when coffee was served. They drank it at the table, with the piano music for a background.

The conversation became lively, with theatrical anecdotes from Jack, a little from Candida about her job as medical secretary to three consultants, and, eventually, with a little persuasion from Jack, a very sketchy account of his occupation from Rhodri. Hilary wasn't in the least surprised to learn he was with a merchant bank. He looked exactly what she expected a merchant banker to look like, and probably rarely did. Prosperous-looking, somehow, she decided secretly. Self-assured and very much master of his own fate. Then her hard-won well-being vanished abruptly when, in response to Rhodri's question, she told him that the library she was bound for was situated in the county of Gwent.

Jack's eyebrows rose. 'You're talking to the right man then, Hilary. That's Rod's own particular little neck of the woods—or used to be.'

'Oh—really?' she said quickly. 'Do—do you go back there much?'

The dismay in her voice was so patent that Candida frowned bleakly at her, and Rhodri's smile was wry.

'Not very often these days. Not since my mother died.' He changed the subject with a firmness which indicated it was one he didn't care to pursue, pressing the others to brandy with their coffee, but excusing himself on the grounds of driving everyone home. His whisky before dinner had been the only drink Rhodri had allowed himself, Hilary noticed, and after the shock of her overdose of gin she'd been equally abstemious herself, refusing the wine Candida and Jack drank with their meal.

Not long afterwards they left the warmth of the hotel's comfortable Gothic interior, to hurry the short distance outside into the Randolph's indoor car-park, where Rhodri led the way to a Jaguar XJ-S convertible with its hood secured in place against the wintry January night.

Candida exchanged a swift, impressed look with Hilary, then tucked herself in the back of the car with Jack, leaving her sister to ride in front with the driver. Hilary, accustomed to the rattles and coughs of her elderly Mini, was lost in admiration at the smoothness of the ride, and the surprising sensation of being insulated from the rest of the world, no draught creeping inside the flexible hood, and very little noise coming from the powerful engine. The short ride was over far too soon for her.

'What a wonderful, wonderful car,' she breathed reverently, as they drew up outside the house where Candida lived.

'And I thought it was fright over my driving that kept you so quiet!' said Rhodri, as he helped her out.

'Not a bit of it. Just sheer appreciation. I've never been this near such an impressive piece of machinery!' Hilary smiled up at him spontaneously in the light of the street lamp, and Rhodri rubbed his chin thoughtfully.

'At last, at last, Hilary Mason.'

She frowned. 'At last what?'

'A real, live smile. Even if it was for my car rather than me.'

'Come on, you two,' said Candida, shivering. 'Let's go and drink lots of coffee. I'm freezing.'

The two men stayed for a companionable half-hour, then Jack repaired to the kitchen to wash up with Candida, leaving Hilary and Rhodri alone for a few minutes.

'Do you think I can consider myself forgiven now?' asked Rhodri, the moment the kitchen door closed on the others.

Hilary's eyes dropped, and she toyed with her locket and chain. 'Oh, please, let's just forget about last night. Anyway, *you* were the injured party, not me.'

He touched a finger to the strip of adhesive plaster on his forehead and smiled at her, his grey eyes gleaming. 'Very true. I'm only just recovering from your attentions! Not the least of which was the humiliation of finding I'd been laid out cold by someone half my size. Now please, don't freeze me to death with those eyes of yours—I promise faithfully never to mention the subject again. Do you visit your sister often?' he added abruptly, surprising her.

'Not very often.' Hilary shrugged a little, regretfully. 'And it's likely to be even less often now I'll be working some distance away.'

'Penafon isn't *that* far from Oxford.'

'I realise that.'

'And you'll have holidays.'

'I shall spend those with my parents in Portugal.'

'In short,' he said drily, 'why don't I shut up and mind my own business?'

Hilary bit her lip. 'I didn't mean to be rude. Really. But you see——' She stopped short, vexed to feel her colour rising again.

'See what?' he prompted, his grey eyes holding hers very steadily.

Hilary opted for candour. 'Well, if you want the truth, I find it hard to believe you're in the least bit interested in coming across *me* again now you've met Candida.'

His rather dark eyebrows met suddenly. 'Are you jealous of your sister?'

'Good heavens, no,' said Hilary, with such obvious truth Rhodri looked at her searchingly. 'Candida can't help being beautiful. And believe me, she possesses a disposition to match her looks. It just isn't possible to feel jealousy or resentment where she's concerned. Which doesn't alter the fact that I'm used to being invisible as far as most men are concerned when she's around. It's part of life.'

'You're entirely wrong——' he began forcibly, then halted. The other two were coming back into the room in the midst of an argument about an old film they'd both seen recently, and the moment of confidence was over.

'Well?' demanded Candida, after the men had taken their leave. 'It wasn't such an ordeal after all, was it? The evening, I mean.'

'No,' admitted Hilary with caution. 'In fact I quite enjoyed parts of it, especially the drive home. What a sensational car!'

'It's got rather a sensational owner, Hilly, in my opinion.'

'More so than Jack?' asked Hilary slyly.

'No. But then, Jack's Jack. Not a type one can compare, really, and why I'm eating my heart out over the wretch I really don't know.' Candida slumped despondently on the sofa. 'It's obvious he just thinks of me as a pal. If anything, I think he talked more to you tonight than to me.'

'Rubbish,' scoffed Hilary. 'If that were all he felt, why would he come here hotfoot to ask you to this première of his?'

Candida turned cynical blue eyes on her sibling. 'Because, my pet, Davy will be there with that gorgeous husband of hers, and Jack, being a male—*and* an actor—wants some protective covering, in the shape of a presentable companion. Which is where I come in. I'm not over-endowed with grey matter, Hilly, but nature gave me a good figure, plus this hair and this face, and if they're the only ammunition I've got I'll use them to the best effect. I'll treat myself to a drop-dead dress and do Jack proud, and everyone will wonder who I am, which is probably exactly what he has in mind.'

Hilary frowned anxiously at the disillusionment in her sister's voice. 'But Candida, I've always so much envied you your looks.'

'I know. And you're an idiot. There's nothing wrong with your own.'

'I don't know about that. Anyway, I could tell that Rhodri Lloyd-Ellis was very taken with you, just like every other man who's ever laid eyes on you.'

'My turn to say rubbish!' Candida bit her lip, hesitating, then she shot a questioning look at Hilary. 'I think you're very taken with *him*, though, aren't you, love?'

Hilary opened her mouth to say no, then smiled wryly. 'Yes. I'm afraid I am, rather.'

'I thought so. I've never seen you so prickly.'

'Well, who wouldn't be after such a catastrophic introduction!'

'Yes. Well——' Candida shrugged. 'The thing is, Hilly, if you do—well—like him, I mean, then we're both in the same boat. It must run in the family.'

Hilary's eyebrows rose. 'What do you mean?'

'Well, Jack makes no bones about still hankering after Davy, and it appears from what he told me while we were in the kitchen to be more than probable his elegant cousin is carrying a torch for some sort of childhood sweetheart who had the bad taste to marry someone else.'

Hilary felt a very sharp pain somewhere in her midriff, survived it, and shrugged carelessly. 'Poor man! Not that it matters to me. I shall be over the hills and far away come tomorrow afternoon. Once I'm stuck in to my new job in Penafon, I won't have time for pipe-dreams about sophisticated merchant bankers. Rhodri Lloyd-Ellis will just be someone I once passed a pleasant evening with— and, far more important, the owner of the most ravishing car I'm ever likely to ride in!'

CHAPTER THREE

PENAFON was a pretty little town, with ruins of a castle from its Border heritage, a square-towered church with gravestones dating back centuries, and very few modern buildings at all. Most of the houses and shops and inns were a conglomeration of several bygone periods, and all of them, it seemed at first glance, had owners who took great pride in keeping their properties spick and span and fresh with paint. Some of the houses were built of grey stone and sported white shutters and green creepers on their walls, others were painted pink or white and picked out in black, and many of them had the sentry-box porches characteristic of the area.

The general effect was one of peace and charm, and Hilary felt a surge of pleasure as she parked her Mini beside the grey stone wall which partly sheltered a surprisingly modern little row of two-storey flats built overlooking the churchyard. A pretty ironwork stair led up to her own flat on the upper floor of the nearest end section, and Hilary struggled up it with a will, laden with bags and packages.

Almost at once a head popped out of the door in the bottom flat, and a pretty, lilting voice called, 'Need a hand?'

Hilary peered down from the minuscule landing outside her own door, shivering in the biting wind coming from the river, which flowed past only a short distance away. A girl with gypsy-black curls smiled up cheerfully in welcome. 'We can supply some muscles, if you like.'

35

Hilary grinned back. 'Yes, please!' She dumped the bags, unlocked her new front door and ran back down the little spiral stair, holding out her hand. 'I'm Hilary Mason.'

'We know that, don't worry!' The other girl's eyes gleamed with mischief. 'Everybody in Penafon knows everything about everyone else. So be warned! I'm Catrin Probert——' She glanced behind her as a squarely-built dark man emerged from the doorway, hurriedly pulling on a heavy sweater. 'And this is my brother Rhys. Come *on*, Rhys—Hilary here needs a hand with all that stuff in her car.'

'How do you do, Miss Mason,' said Rhys Probert, ignoring his exuberant young sister. 'Welcome to Penafon.'

Hilary took his hand, smiling a little shyly. 'Thank you.' She rather liked the look of the broad-shouldered man with the bruising handshake. He had dark curly hair like his sister, and heavy eyebrows over deep-set dark eyes.

'Right then,' he said briskly. 'Let's get your belongings up that idiotic little staircase, and don't catch your heel in the ironwork, Miss Mason.'

Catrin promptly insisted on first names, and dispelled any shyness on Hilary's part by chattering away nineteen to the dozen as the three of them hauled the contents of the Mini up the staircase and into the flat. The furniture and tea-chests delivered the week before had been stacked in the kitchen and the living-room, according to labels, except for the bed, which the removal people had set up in the small room overlooking the pretty little street. Hilary had labelled all her boxes neatly before the removal men collected them from the family home in Warwickshire, when she had helped supervise the distribution of her parents' belongings, some of it into storage, some to Candida's house in Oxford, and the rest to 1A Glebe Row in Penafon.

'Before we make a start on this lot,' said Catrin, 'I vote you come downstairs and have some coffee to warm you up. Have you had lunch?'

'I stopped on my way,' said Hilary quickly. 'But coffee would be wonderful.'

The flat below was colourful with bright rugs and curtains and plants overflowing every window-sill, and a general air of welcome to match its vivacious young owner. While the three of them drank large mugs of very good coffee dispensed from the new brass cafetière Catrin said she'd been given as a moving-in present, Hilary learnt that her lively young neighbour worked as a secretary for a firm of architects in Newport.

'Rhys is one of them,' she said, pulling a face. 'Only there's no nepotism about it, I can tell you. He works me to death.'

Rhys Probert leaned back on the small, comfortable sofa, smiling at Hilary. 'She means I make sure she earns the very respectable wage we pay her. Which, I may add, has made this flat possible.'

Catrin nodded, laughing. 'Yes. I've actually been allowed to fly the nest! My parents took a lot of persuading, but I won in the end. Mainly because Rhys heard of this place in Penafon. They can't imagine anything untoward happening to me here, because it's such a nice, respectable little town.'

'Don't you find it a long way to travel?' asked Hilary curiously. 'One of the attractions of the job in the library here was the fact that I'd be able to walk to work every day.' She smiled at the other two. 'I assume you knew I was the new librarian?'

'Of course!' said Rhys drily. 'Catrin's been here a mere month, but she could have given you a complete rundown on the intimate details of Penafon society after the first weekend.'

'I'm not as bad as that!' Catrin jumped to her feet. 'Anyway, Rhys Probert, I'm sure a couple of hours putting up shelves for me hasn't worn you out. Let's go up to 1A and help Hilary arrange her furniture.'

'It's very kind of you, but I'm sure I can manage if you're busy,' said Hilary quickly.

Her protests were swept summarily aside, and within a surprisingly short time 1A Glebe Row began to feel very much like home to Hilary, as Rhys Probert's muscular strength made short work of moving chairs and tables and the heavy oak bureau that had once stood in the Masons' hall at home. Only *this* was now home, Hilary reminded herself. Home for her parents was in future a villa in the Algarve, where her father's weak chest could benefit from the warm climate, and her mother could stop worrying about him so much. And, in the meantime, the little flat soon began to look quite lived-in, with Hilary's own brass bed in the bedroom, and her mother's carpet and sofa and chairs in the small sitting-room which looked out on a strip of garden with a glimpse of the river beyond.

'I really am grateful,' said Hilary, when she felt it was time to call a halt. 'I never expected help, you know. You've both been wonderfully kind.'

'Nonsense,' said Rhys, resuming his sweater. He grinned. 'Catrin's been dying to meet her new neighbour—she's been on the look-out for you all morning, instead of giving me a hand.'

Catrin gave him a sisterly shove. 'Don't let him worry you, Hilary. I'm not here in the daytime during the week, and you can always tell me to push off if I poke my nose in too often when I am here.'

Hilary shook her head, smiling. 'I can't see that happening, somehow.'

'You don't really know her yet,' warned Rhys darkly, and glanced at his watch. 'I vote we repair to the Afon Arms and see if they'll provide us with a bar snack. All this exercise has given me an appetite.'

Thus it was that Hilary found herself, for the second night running, dining with a new male acquaintance. Catrin and Rhys were easy, congenial company in the comfortable surroundings of the Afon Arms, which was the focal point of the town, and had been a celebrated coaching inn in the days when horsepower had been a literal description of the only means of transport on the roads of Monmouthshire, as it was then. The town was a favourite spot for keen fishermen at weekends, Hilary was told, and in summer Penafon was very much busier than at present, with visitors who flocked to see the show of flowers which the inhabitants took pride in planting in hanging baskets, window boxes, gardens, and even in containers attached to the wrought-iron lamps along the bridge spanning the river which ran through the town.

'I think I'm going to like it here,' Hilary said contentedly, as she drank a glass of lager.

'A shade quiet for a girl like you,' commented Rhys. He leaned back in his chair, looking at her.

'Oh, I'm all for a quiet life,' said Hilary lightly, aware that Catrin was watching her brother with bright, speculative eyes.

'If you get bored you can always sample the social delights of Newport and Cardiff,' he said. 'The New Theatre there's been reopened. They get West End plays sometimes before they open in London. And there's the Welsh National Opera, of course.'

'Rhys likes opera,' said Catrin, and fixed her brother
with a very straight look. 'I don't think Lynne does,
though, does she?'

Rhys downed the rest of his beer and stood up. 'No,'
he said shortly, 'she doesn't. Right then, ladies. I'll see
you back to your respective abodes, then I must be off.
Early start in the morning.'

When they were back in Catrin's flat, and Rhys had
made his farewells, Catrin insisted Hilary had another
coffee before going off to bed.

'I felt I had to mention Lynne,' said Catrin awkwardly. 'She's Rhys's girlfriend.'

Hilary grinned. 'I rather gathered that.'

'Well, he tends to forget her existence sometimes when
he meets a pretty girl like you. I wouldn't want you to—
to misunderstand, or anything.'

'Oh, I won't!' Hilary assured her as she got up to go,
much cheered by the term 'pretty girl'. 'It's remarkably
rare to meet an attractive man who *doesn't* have a girl
already in tow. Or who doesn't hanker after some other
woman,' she added morosely, thinking of both Jack and
Rhodri.

'Do you have a boyfriend?' asked Catrin.

'No. Do you?'

'Loads of them. Safety in numbers—that's my motto!'

Which was probably a good idea, thought Hilary later,
as she made her way up the spiral stair to her new front
door. Candida had made it *her* motto, goodness knows,
over the years, which still hadn't prevented her from
falling for a man who was in love with someone else.
As she unlocked her door Hilary could hear her new
telephone ringing. After a moment to remember where
she'd put it, she dashed for her bedside table and picked
up the receiver.

'Where have you been?' demanded Candida, aggrieved.

Hilary explained. 'Anyway, I said I'd ring at ten in case you went out,' she added, and glanced at her watch. 'I'm only five minutes overdue.'

Candida was quickly appeased when she heard about Hilary's friendly young neighbour, and the large, helpful brother who'd been so efficient with the furniture-shifting.

'*And* he took us both for a bar meal at the local hostelry, after which he zoomed off in his very nice black BMW and I've come back to make up my chaste little bed so I can fall on it and get a good night's sleep, ready for my first day at Penafon Library.'

Candida was obviously relieved to hear her little sister was happy in her new home, then went on to say Jack Wynne Jones had called round to take her out to lunch, and make arrangements for the première of his film.

'Wonderful!' cried Hilary. 'I'm so pleased.'

'Personally I'd be rather more pleased myself if I didn't think his main purpose had been to get your address, Hilly.'

Hilary blinked in astonishment. '*My* address? You're joking. Why on earth should he want that?'

'It's a question that's been buzzing round in my brain ever since he left,' said Candida drily, and went on to give a lot of sisterly instruction on eating properly and being friendly to the locals, and generally taking care.

Hilary giggled and told her sister to stop being such a fusspot, then said goodnight and began to push her quilt into a clean cover, wondering why on earth Jack should be interested in where *she* lived. She shrugged, and forgot about it as she settled herself for sleep in her new bedroom, just slightly apprehensive about her first day in a new job.

*   *   *

Hilary's misgivings about her colleagues and her job proved unnecessary. The other women, mainly married part-timers, were very friendly and helpful, and the building itself, once a small primary school, had been modernised in sympathy with its age, and was a very pleasant place to pass the working day.

The finishing touch to Hilary's happy first day was provided by the large cardboard box she found sitting at the top of the spiral stair outside her new front door when she got home. She rushed inside the flat with it and tore open the box eagerly, to find an azalea in a white porcelain pot. The card with it said, 'Happy homecoming. Rhodri.'

Hilary subsided on a kitchen stool, gazing open-mouthed at the plant's delicate white blossom. Utterly astonishing though it might be, it would seem that her address had been for Rhodri, then, not his cousin!

Candida tried hard not to sound jubilant when Hilary rang her with the news later, but it was obvious she was deeply relieved. Jealousy of her young sister would be a very new emotion in Candida's life, Hilary knew, and she was only too pleased to tell her it was unnecessary.

Candida sighed. 'It's galling to admit it, but I hardly slept last night, wondering why Jack wanted your address, and telling myself how noble I would have to be if he preferred you to me.'

'Now, is that likely?'

'Very. Jack thinks you're sweet.'

'Yuck!'

'Sweet's what the man said. Anyway, how did your day go?'

Hilary told her it had gone very well indeed.

And in time she found every day went just as well. The citizens of Penafon were in the main very friendly and pleasant, teasing her a little because she was a 'foreigner', but generally making her feel welcome in their community. She went to church most Sunday mornings, and had a drink with Catrin in one of the pubs some evenings. On weekends she sometimes went to the cinema in Newport, weather permitting, but a fall of snow during February discouraged her for a while from driving very far.

There was really only one fly in the ointment. Two flies, she added to herself, if she were entirely honest. One was the struggle she had to make ends meet, because 1A Glebe Row was rather a luxury for a girl living on her particular modest stipend. The other was the fact that the azalea had been the only communication from Rhodri Lloyd-Ellis. It had been a one-off friendly gesture, she told herself stoically. And since her own response had been a very formal card of printed thanks, with only her signature to personalise it, there was no point at all in complaining because she'd heard nothing more from him. But secretly she couldn't help feeling disappointed, however firmly her brain insisted its owner had more sense than to expect someone of Rhodri's age and sophistication, a man with such elegant good looks and assurance—not to mention such a car, she added, sighing—to give much thought to someone like herself.

Hilary took to examining her face in the mirror, trying to see it objectively. There was nothing wrong with it. She had a short nose, sprinkled with a few faint freckles, admittedly, but it was straight, and her skin was clear these days, and her eyes were as satisfactory as any girl could want. She'd let her hair grow a little longer, and one day had given in to temptation and let the local hairdresser add one or two fair streaks which looked rather good. Catrin had been ecstatic. Rhys had been less effusive, but a certain look in his eye had made it plain he agreed with his sister.

In a way, of course, Rhys Probert could almost be termed the third fly in her ointment. Hilary frowned. A couple of weeks earlier Catrin's car had broken down and needed what its owner had described gloomily as major surgery. As a result Rhys had taken to running his sister home at night, and staying for the evening sometimes to persuade both girls out for a meal. It seemed silly to refuse, when he never tried to corner her on her own, but Hilary couldn't rid herself of the feeling that in some way Rhys Probert was biding his time as far as she was concerned.

Then, late one evening, Hilary and Catrin were watching a theatre awards ceremony on television together when Rhys came hammering on the door.

'What on earth are you doing here at this time of night?' demanded his sister, as she let him in.

'I've been up at Cwmderwen Court Hotel,' he said, shaking the rain from his hair as he closed the door behind him. 'Make me some coffee, there's a good girl.'

'Were our plans accepted for the new bedroom wing?' called Catrin as she made a fresh pot.

'No,' said Rhys blackly. 'I need cheering up, I'm afraid. Apparently someone else's design was considered more suitable.' He shrugged. 'You win some, you lose some. Anyway, the hotel will be needing some new staff pretty soon, which isn't a bad thing locally. Should be plenty of would-be aspirants for jobs.'

'Part-time as well as full-time?' asked Hilary thoughtfully.

'I should think so.' He looked at her curiously. 'Why? Are you thinking of leaving the library?'

'No, of course not. But I finish at midday on Saturdays. If they need extra weekend help I might apply.' Hilary laughed at the appalled look on both dark Probert faces. 'Don't look so shocked. I need the money.'

'Have you eaten tonight?' demanded Rhys fiercely.

'I didn't say I was starving! Merely that a little extra pocket-money would be welcome to pay the electricity bill, etc.' Hilary was sorry she'd brought the subject up. Catrin looked worried to death.

'If you're ever really short——' the girl began urgently.

'I apply to my parents,' said Hilary, and smiled reassuringly. 'But I've no intention of doing that if I can help it.'

It was so late by the time Rhys and Catrin stopped bombarding her with offers of help that the former decided he'd spend the night on his sister's sofa rather than brave the elements on the journey back to Newport. He insisted on escorting Hilary up the spiral outside stair to see her safely inside her flat.

'Thank you,' said Hilary, and smiled at him. 'Quite unnecessary, but very nice of you to make sure no one was lurking in the shadows.'

'I came up because I wanted to kiss you goodnight,' he said bluntly, and promptly acted on his words, taking her breath away. When he raised his head he stared down into her startled eyes. 'Are you going to slap my face?'

Hilary detached herself from his embrace, trying for lightness. 'A bit out of date, I think. But, just the same, I'd rather you didn't make a habit of it.'

'Why?' His black brows rose quizzically.

'Various reasons. One of which, surely, must be the fact that—that someone else probably considers she has a monopoly on your kisses.'

'And if there weren't someone else?' he demanded.

'Since there is,' said Hilary lightly, 'I think you'd better go back downstairs, or Catrin will be worried.'

'Furious, more likely. She's a proper little spitfire when she loses her temper.'

'So am I,' Hilary warned him. 'Goodnight, Rhys.'

He gave her a mocking grin and ducked back out into the black, wet night, leaving her very thoughtful as she got ready for bed. She had quite enjoyed the unexpected kiss. More, if she were truthful, than any other kiss she'd ever had. But then, Rhys Probert was a very attractive man. Yet, as she turned out the light, Hilary found herself wondering what it would be like to be kissed by Rhodri Lloyd-Ellis, which was a great mistake, since the thought kept her awake for half the night.

Next day marked the occasion of her first trip with the mobile library van. Her driver was Evan Richards, a retired policeman much respected locally, who knew the surrounding countryside like the back of his hand, and Hilary thoroughly enjoyed meeting the mainly elderly people who awaited her arrival eagerly. She was touched that they so plainly relished their little chat with her as she helped choose their books. Her route took her to outlying farms, through neighbourhoods where public transport was scarce, and Evan was a mine of interesting information on the area as they went along. Hilary fell deeper in love with rural Gwent with every mile, and looked forward to summer, picturing the countryside's bare winter charm transformed into the green glow of summer.

A sharp wind eddied along Glebe Row as Hilary hurried along it on her way home, making her eyes smart as they widened at the sight of a dark car parked near the lych-gate of the church, its long, low shape unmistakable in the light of one of the Victorian street lamps which Penafon took pride in keeping to light some of the older streets. Hilary's jaw dropped as she recognised Rhodri's convertible, her eyes widening even more as Rhodri's tall, limber figure swung itself out of the car, hand held out in greeting as he smiled down into her astonished face.

'Hello, Hilary Mason. As I was in the neighbourhood I thought I'd come and see how you were settling in.'

Hilary swallowed. 'Good heavens, what a surprise!' She took his hand, wishing her own were encased in something more elegant than a woollen mitten, then pulled herself together, and smiled back, gesturing towards the spiral stair leading to her flat, glad that for once there were no lights in Catrin's windows. 'If you feel like braving my stairs I'll give you some coffee or a drink.'

Rhodri shook his head. 'I don't think that's wise, Hilary, not in a place like Penafon.'

'As you wish, of course,' she said stiffly, and Rhodri's grasp tightened on the hand he still held.

'Don't be offended. Please.' His face sobered. 'Remember I was brought up in a place rather similar to this. Everyone is usually privy to everyone else's affairs, and if Miss Mason the new librarian were known to be entertaining a strange man in her flat the whole town would be agog with it before you could say knife.'

Hilary bit her lip, eyeing him uncertainly. 'I suppose you're right.' She was glad of the darkness which hid her sudden colour as she remembered Rhys Probert's lack of scruples on the same subject a short while before. 'So. It's hello and goodbye, then.'

'I hope *not*,' he said, with flattering emphasis. 'I've come quite a bit out of my way to see you, Hilary. Won't you at least reward me with your company over dinner?'

Hilary could hardly believe her ears. Rhodri Lloyd-Ellis had actually travelled miles specifically to see *her*? 'It's a bit early,' she said diffidently.

'I'll take myself off to the bar of the Afon Arms and read the paper while I have a drink, then in an hour or so I'll come back and collect you.' Rhodri released her hand and bent to peer into her face. 'Well? Will you, Hilary?'

'Thank you. I'd like that very much,' she said, wondering wildly whether an hour would give her time to wash her hair, not to mention all sorts of other things necessary to make herself presentable enough for dinner with Rhodri Lloyd-Ellis.

'In an hour, then,' he said, getting into the car. He leaned to look at her through the open window. 'And don't be late. I'm hungry. Oh, by the way,' he added, 'remind me to give you various messages Candida made me promise to pass on to you verbatim.'

CHAPTER FOUR

HILARY'S enthusiasm for the evening evaporated into thin air as she watched the spectacular car purr away. All, it seemed, was revealed. Rhodri's reason for looking her up was simple. Candida had asked him to, and, what was more, had omitted to say anything about it during her most recent telephone chat.

Oh, well, thought Hilary philosophically, at least it was another free meal to help with her budget, which was turning out to be rather more tight than anticipated when she originally leapt at the offer of the job. Of course, it was Candida who'd insisted she splash out on the little flat, rather than live in lodgings with one of Penafon's hospitable matrons. More privacy and freedom, she'd said. Hilary smiled wryly, as she lay in the bath. Little Candida knew about it. Rhodri, on the other hand, seemed very well-versed in the ways of a town like Penafon. Unless, of course, the unvarnished truth was that he just hadn't fancied a cosy interlude up there with her in her little retreat.

Hilary dressed with care in a grey flannel skirt and a gentian-blue mohair sweater Candida had knitted for her, grinning as she remembered the latter's pleas never to say a word on pain of death about Candida's quite exceptional talent for knitting—a revelation Candida was convinced would ruin her image. With regard to her own image, Hilary used up most of her precious hour in twisting her newly washed hair into a complicated upswept knot to make herself look older, but felt quite pleased with her reflection when the expected knock came on her door at the exact moment her allotted time expired. Rhodri must be hungry, she thought as she shrugged on her grey flannel blazer and flung on a long blue scarf.

'I'm ready,' she said briskly, and flung open the door, then stopped dead. Instead of Rhodri's elegant presence she was confronted with the broad-shouldered figure of Rhys Probert.

'So I see,' he said softly, eyeing her with speculation. 'Ready for what? I wonder.'

'I'm going out, Rhys.' Hilary smiled, but deliberately made no move to invite him in.

'Who with?' he demanded.

'A friend. So unless there's something I can do for you I'm afraid I'll have to let you go, or I'll be late.'

'I came to see if you'd care to come downstairs for supper, Hilary, but it seems I've been beaten to the tape.' He sighed dramatically. 'Ah, me! I'll go and tell Catrin it's just the two of us for *cawl* after all.'

'Sorry, Rhys. Tell Catrin I'd love to come and eat *cawl*—whatever that is, some other time,' said Hilary, wishing Rhys would make himself scarce quickly.

'All right, love. I can see you're like a cat on hot bricks so I'll disappear like the lamb I am.' His smile had more of the wolf than the lamb about it as he ran down the spiral stair just as the Jaguar convertible drew up at the foot of it. Rhys turned to wave up at Hilary very deliberately, then disappeared through Catrin's door as Rhodri emerged from the car. Hilary angrily banged her own door shut and went slowly down the stairs, mindful of her high heels on the ironwork.

'Hello,' she said, and smiled at Rhodri, who was gazing very thoughtfully in the direction of the ground-floor flat. 'I thought I'd be ready and waiting so you didn't have to sully my fair name by even knocking on my door.'

'Unlike your neighbour—who seems unburdened by similar scruples,' said Rhodri softly.

'He's my neighbour's *brother*, to be precise, and he doesn't live in Penafon.'

'And does he make a habit of calling on you alone?'

'Not that it's any of your business,' retorted Hilary coldly, 'but in actual fact he doesn't. He was delivering an invitation to supper with his sister.'

Rhodri opened the car door with a slight bow. 'In which case I was fortunate to be the early bird, it seems.'

His face was so cold with disapproval that for two pins Hilary would have told him to forget the whole idea of an evening together, but Catrin's curtains were twitching, and sheer feminine pride made it impossible to do anything other than get in the car.

'Perhaps we should start all over again,' said Rhodri, as they drove off. 'Good evening, Hilary, how very charming you look.'

'Good evening, Rhodri. Thank you,' she replied in kind, and gave him a wry, sidelong glance. The chilly wind had ruffled his fair hair, making him look less faultlessly perfect in the deliciously leather-scented darkness of the car as they travelled the brief distance to the hotel.

'I'm sorry, Hilary. I had no right to make snide comments about your friends.' He turned the Jaguar into the car park of the Afon Arms and switched off the ignition, turning in his seat to smile at her crookedly. 'Only it rather got me on the raw to find some chap running down your stairs when I'd so nobly refrained from climbing *up* them earlier on just for the sake of your reputation!'

Hilary looked at him soberly, then shrugged. 'If it's any consolation to you, Rhys didn't come inside either.'

Rhodri gave her a very unsettling smile. 'You know, I rather think it is, Hilary.'

Uncertain how to respond to that, Hilary turned away to open the car door, and stood beside it, shivering, as Rhodri locked up before taking her arm to hurry her inside to the warmth of the bar. The head waiter swiftly relieved them of their coats, showed them to a small table at one of the windows in the bar, produced large, ornate menus for them to study at their leisure, then sent the barman to take their orders for drinks.

'My goodness,' said Hilary, impressed. 'I'm not used to such attention.'

'You've been here before, surely?' asked Rhodri.

'Several times, but only to a snack meal here in the bar.' She smiled at him demurely. 'I've never aspired to the glories of the dining-room proper.'

'I only hope you won't be disappointed. I haven't eaten a meal here for years.' Rhodri scanned the delights on offer, and advised some of the salmon the hotel offered as a speciality. 'Straight from the river outside, with luck,' he said with a grin, and gave serious consideration to the wine list. 'Their cellar here has a good reputation. Have you any particular preference?'

'I know nothing at all about it,' she said honestly, 'except that I prefer it to be white, and not excessively dry.'

The waiter interrupted eagerly, with the information that, if the gentleman wished, the cellar had a Château d'Yquem of the very best quality Sauternes, and—a dramatic pause—of the 1967 vintage. Hilary's eyes started out of her head at the price, which the waiter referred to as a *little* bit high, but by no means unreasonable.

'You'll like it,' Rhodri assured her, laughter in his eyes at her expression.

'I wouldn't dare do anything else!' She frowned at him. 'Surely something less extravagant would have done just as well?'

'It isn't often one's offered something so fine, particularly in a fairly remote place like this.' He shrugged. 'It seemed a crime to turn down the chance.' He leaned forward to look very squarely into her face. 'What's going on behind those extraordinary blue eyes of yours, I wonder?'

Hilary looked at him consideringly, at the jacket cut by some inspired designer's hand, at his shirt which, at a guess, was probably made for him, as were the shoes on his long, elegant feet, even to the discipline of his thick, ash-blond hair, which was obviously the result of a master's craft.

'I was wondering,' she said slowly, twirling her sherry glass, 'what it must be like to be able to order wine like that without a second thought.'

'You disapprove?' he said swiftly.

'Oh, no. It was purely an academic exercise.' Hilary smiled cheerfully. 'Believe me, I'm not knocking it— and there was nothing deprived about my childhood. But my father taught Classics to unwilling schoolboys, so there was never much spare cash in our household. Then my mother, amazingly, won some money with Premium Bonds, which is why they were able to retire to Portugal.'

'You miss them, I expect.' His voice deepened with sympathy.

'Oh, I do, but I'm very glad for them. Father badly needed a warmer, drier climate for his chest.'

'And you can always fly over to see them whenever you want.'

Not quite, thought Hilary ruefully. Air fares were a luxury she couldn't afford for the present.

They were installed in the comfort of the discreetly lit hotel dining-room, and were beginning on the salmon prepared with grapes and champagne before Rhodri reverted to the subject of money.

'I suppose I can be described as comfortably off,' he said, filling Hilary's wine glass, once the ritual of tasting had been accomplished to the waiter's satisfaction. 'But only materially. I have a highly paid job I enjoy, my house in Oxford, and a bit of other property, but no family closer than Jack and his clan, other than a few distant connections on my mother's side. I was an only child, my parents are dead, and the only lady I ever remotely considered marrying very sensibly chose someone far more exciting than me.'

Which only demonstrated her extraordinary lack of taste, thought Hilary, and sipped the wine with caution.

'Well?' asked Rhodri, grinning. 'What's the verdict?'

'I told you I'm not qualified to give an opinion, but for what it's worth I think it's utterly sensational.' Hilary raised her glass to him. 'Thank you for the experience, Rhodri.'

He returned the salute gravely. 'Only the first of many such, I trust.'

What did he mean by that? That he hoped she'd find other wines as wonderful in future, or that he himself hoped to provide them? Hilary applied herself to the salmon, damped down suddenly as she remembered he'd mentioned Candida earlier on.

'By the way, what are these messages you had from my sister?' she asked lightly, keeping her eyes on her plate.

'I must confess that I haven't actually seen Candida myself. Jack relayed them to me, so if they lose something in transit blame him.' Rhodri chuckled, and Hilary looked up with a smile of such involuntary radiance he looked stunned. 'Good lord,' he breathed, transfixed. 'Why don't you do that more often?'

'I'll try,' she said pertly, filled with elation. 'Anyway, what did my big sister have to say?'

Rhodri's eyes narrowed as he tried to remember the list of instructions from Candida, who required to know whether Hilary was eating properly, was she warm enough in her flat, was it in a nice location, was she happy in her job, and was Penafon really as pleasant a place as Hilary made it out to be?

'Oh, really!' said Hilary, laughing. 'She's the limit. How the soul of a mother-hen manages to hide behind that amazing exterior of hers I'll never know. I've told her all that over and over again on the telephone.'

Rhodri pushed aside his plate and leaned his chin on his hands, his eyes dancing. 'Don't tell me that your breathtaking sister is really earth mother in disguise!'

'She is, you know. All that exterior gloss and frivolity is nothing to do with the real Candida.' Hilary lowered her voice and leaned nearer. 'She'd kill me if she knew I'd told you, but she actually made the jersey I'm wearing. She's an amazing cook, too. Our genes got terribly mixed up somewhere. I look as though all I *do* is knit and cook, and so on, whereas all I ever really want to do is read, read, read. And Candida, who looks like the original party-girl, would like nothing better than a husband and a houseful of children she could feed—and clothe in hand-knitted woollies.'

Rhodri threw back his head and roared with laughter, which turned several heads towards them in curiosity. 'Does Jack realise all this?' he demanded.

'You won't tell him!' said Hilary in alarm. 'Please, Rhodri, don't breathe a word, or she'll rend me limb from limb. Candida would hate someone of Jack's type to suspect she was anything but what she appears.'

'Jack's type,' said Rhodri thoughtfully. 'What do you mean by that?'

'Star of stage, screen and television and all that. A celebrity. The last man in the world to fancy domesticity and muddy wellingtons, *et al.*'

They were interrupted by the waiter, who wished to know whether they preferred their coffee at their table or in the bar. Rhodri gave a quick glance around the now deserted room, and smiled questioningly at Hilary.

'Shall we stay where we are?'

She nodded, and they were left alone to enjoy their coffee in complete solitude. They were seated opposite each other on high-backed settles which, now the room was empty of diners, formed a little island of privacy that Hilary found disturbingly intimate.

'I never did find out how you happen to be in this part of the world,' she said, shy under the intent grey gaze trained on her face.

'Just attending to some of the property I spoke about. It's more than likely I'll be in the area quite often for a while.' He reached out a hand to touch hers. 'Perhaps we could do this again some time.'

Hilary raised her head to look at him. 'If you like.'

'I like very much.' There was no smile in the grey eyes now. They held a light quite unlike the laughter of minutes before. 'Next time it might be better if I rang beforehand to make sure you're free. One of the things Jack couldn't remember—he who reels off Shakespearian verse by the yard—was your phone number, so I chanced my luck tonight. In the nick of time, as it happened.'

'I don't go out that much.'

'Perhaps you'll let me remedy that.'

Their eyes met and held, and only the arrival of the head waiter, discreetly proffering the bill, broke the spell. After Rhodri had settled up he took Hilary's jacket from the waiter and helped her into it in the foyer, winding her scarf about her neck as though she were a little girl.

'It's cold out there tonight,' he said softly, and, bemused, Hilary smiled up at him. As he shrugged himself into an ancient waxed jacket her eyes were drawn past him to meet the brooding black gaze of Rhys Probert, who stood propped against the bar, watching them. Hilary smiled, but a sardonic nod was her only response, and she turned away quickly, unwilling to let Rhys's hostile presence spoil the evening for her.

'Wasn't that your visitor of earlier on?' asked Rhodri, as he took her hand to run with her to the car.

'Yes,' gasped Hilary, her breath taken away by the icy wind howling up from the river.

Rhodri unlocked the car and quickly helped her inside, then slid in beside her. The car park was deserted, and there was no one to see when he leaned towards her and touched his lips very gently to her cheek. 'Thank you for taking pity on my solitary state tonight, Hilary.'

'I should be thanking you,' she retorted. 'For the dinner, and that miraculous wine. It was all perfect.'

'So it was. The company most of all,' he said, and bent lower and kissed her lips.

Hilary sat perfectly still, aware in every fibre of the feel of his mouth on hers. The kiss was over long before she wanted it to be as Rhodri drew away, touching a hand to her cheek as he sat upright, and her whole body tingled from the contact, her heart beating in a heavy, thumping way she had never experienced before. Suddenly there was the snarl of an engine close at hand, and lights blazed in their faces as a car Hilary knew to be Rhys Probert's BMW swept past them so close that he narrowly avoided contact with the Jaguar as he roared out of the car park.

Rhodri swore under his breath and took Hilary's hand in his. 'Did that lunatic frighten you, little one? Your pulse is going nineteen to the dozen.'

'No—no, I'm fine. I was a bit startled, that's all.' Not that Rhys Probert was to blame for the rate of her pulse.

The journey back to her flat was much too brief for Hilary. When Rhodri brought the convertible to a halt at the foot of her spiral stair she was conscious of a yearning to prolong the evening, to have him stay instead of leaving her.

'You're not driving back to Oxford tonight?' she said suddenly, feeling anxious at the mere thought of him speeding along a motorway in the powerful car.

'No. I'm putting up at the Afon Arms. But I'll be off at the crack of dawn—should be in the City by mid-morning.' He held out his hand. 'Give me your keys, Miss Mason. I'll escort you up that rickety-looking stair, then make sure you're safely inside your own front door before I go.'

When they reached her door Rhodri unlocked it, then Hilary switched on the lights and turned to smile at him.

'There. No intruders. Goodnight, and thanks once more. It's been a lovely evening.'

The light streamed out on to the little landing, gleaming on Rhodri's fair head, and emphasising the gleam in his eyes as he smiled at her. 'I'll ring you.'

She nodded. 'I'll look forward to it.'

He glanced around him ruefully. 'I feel like a goldfish in a bowl up here.' He held out his hand, and she put hers into it. His fingers tightened as he looked down at her in a way Hilary knew quite well meant he wanted to kiss her again, and something told her that if he did it might not be as gentle as the first time. 'I'd better say goodnight,' he said huskily.

Hilary smiled at him with the wholehearted radiance which had struck him so forcibly earlier. 'Goodnight, Rhodri.'

Involuntarily he bent nearer, then breathed in deeply and gave her a very crooked smile as he dropped her hand and turned away to run down the iron stair, his footsteps loud in the quiet night. As he reached the foot Rhodri looked up at her and waved, then got in the car and drove off, leaving Hilary standing forlornly on her little balcony, watching the Jaguar's tail lights out of sight.

'Who do you think you are?' she asked herself crossly. 'Juliet?' And she went in and closed the door and hurried off to bed, certain she'd lie awake all night reliving the events of the evening in every detail. It was almost an embarrassment next morning when she woke to realise she'd fallen asleep the moment her head touched the pillow, and she laughed at herself sheepishly as she got ready for her working day.

The staff at the library were fully stretched, as it happened, because one of their number was away with flu, and Hilary had no time to daydream. But she was quieter than usual, which gave rise to a little kind questioning from Olwen Hughes, one of the younger married part-timers.

'Feeling all right, Hilary?' she asked in an undertone, in a lull between stamping books and tidying shelves, and dealing with the many and varied enquiries that were part of the job.

Hilary put down the phone after doing her best to enlighten a lady asking about the rateable value of local property, and nodded, smiling. 'I need some coffee, that's all.'

They went together to the back room for a break, as a couple of colleagues took over from them at the counter.

'Phew!' said Olwen, as she made two mugs of strong instant coffee. 'I almost came to blows just now with old Mrs Pugh from Velindre House. She swore blind the wrong date had been stamped on her stack of books. I had to be very firm to get my few pence off her, the old besom, and her rolling in money!'

Hilary laughed, and sat down at the table, sipping her coffee gratefully. 'The richer they are, the less they like parting with the pence, Olwen.'

Olwen nodded absently, studying Hilary's face. 'I heard you were in the Afon Arms last night,' she said casually.

Hilary grinned at her. 'Did you now? It's not the first time, Mrs Hughes. I've been there several times.'

'But not with the man you were dining with last night, my lovely!' Olwen leaned nearer, her dark eyes sparkling. 'I was talking to Damien Jenkins on the way to work—he's my friend Gwyneth's boy, and he works behind the bar at the Afon Arms.'

Hilary laughed. 'Ah, I see.'

'He said the new librarian was having dinner with Mr Lloyd-Ellis who used to live at Cwmderwen Court.'

Hilary frowned. The name had a familiar ring. 'Isn't that the place that's a hotel now?'

'That's right. When Lady Marian died——'

'*Who?*'

Olwen smiled smugly. 'The mother of your friend, Rhodri Lloyd-Ellis!'

Hilary coughed as a mouthful of coffee went down the wrong way. 'But if she was *Lady* Marian——' she spluttered.

'That's right. Daughter of an earl, I believe. Not much money but bags of breeding. It was old Mr Lloyd-Ellis who had the cash. Although,' added Olwen thoughtfully, 'couldn't have been all that much, for Rhodri to sell his home when his mother died.'

If Hilary had been slightly abstracted before the coffee break, her manner for the rest of the day could only be described as dazed. Half of her automatically went on performing her usual function behind the library counter or putting stacks of books away on the shelves, even indulging in conversation with her colleagues and the borrowers who came and went in droves all day. But the other half spent the entire day coming to grips with the fact that any feelings she nurtured for Rhodri would be better stifled at birth.

Her own pedigree was nothing to be ashamed of, it was true—yeomen farmers on the distaff side, and a line of educationists on the other. But the grandson of an earl was a different kettle of fish entirely, and she had no intention of getting involved, however impoverished the said earl might have been. It smacked too much of the squire and the village maiden altogether, for Hilary's taste. Rhodri had been excessively proper about not risking her reputation in Penafon, admittedly, but that was probably because he felt her livelihood depended on it. But something in the way he'd kissed her indicated that if they met in somewhat less inhibiting surroundings his behaviour might be different. And Hilary had no illusions about her response if Rhodri ever did decide to make love to her. Even thinking about it sent her pulse racing, and made the blood leap to her veins. In which case the only sensible thing was to discourage any further meetings—should, of course, he suggest them, she reminded herself. In any case the gap between them was too wide. Thirty-five and twenty, merchant banker and very new librarian—the stuff of dreams, even fantasy, my girl, she told herself sternly. You can forget about Rhodri Lloyd-Ellis as soon as you like; he's definitely not for you.

CHAPTER FIVE

'WHAT rot!' scoffed Candida, when Hilary phoned her the moment she got back to her flat that evening. 'Does it matter if Rhodri was born with a silver spoon in his mouth? If you fancy him, what difference does it make?'

'A lot,' said Hilary flatly. 'If you must know, I felt he was slightly above my touch before, since he's so—so sort of polished and elegant, not to mention years older than me. But with blue blood on top of it——'

'Rubbish, girl! All that went out of date with the bustle.' Candida went on at length on the subject, and demanded a detailed account of the evening with Rhodri, which Hilary obligingly provided, up to a point.

'So when are you seeing him again?' demanded Candida.

Hilary admitted Rhodri had said he'd ring, but infuriated her sister by saying she had no intention of getting in any deeper, then stemmed the flood of scolding by asking about Jack. Jack, it seemed, after entertaining Candida right royally at the première, had dashed up to Oxford a couple of times since to see her, but was at present so busy rehearsing for his West End opening in a new Tom Stoppard play that he had no time for anything else.

'Exit Jack into the sunset, I expect,' said Candida with gloom.

'My turn to say rubbish,' said Hilary, laughing, and said her goodbyes as she rang off to answer a knock on her door.

Catrin burst in, her pretty face bright with curiosity about the handsome driver of the *fabulous* car she'd seen by frankly spying through her window the night before.

'Tell all, *cariad*!' she demanded. 'How come you know Rhodri Lloyd-Ellis? Because that's who Rhys said he was.'

'He's the cousin of a friend of my sister's,' said Hilary. 'Does Rhys know him, then?'

'Knows *of* him. He used to be a big wheel in these parts, but he's something big in the City these days, isn't he?' Catrin looked even more curious as Hilary nodded. 'Rhys was a bit down in the mouth because you didn't come to supper last night. He really fancies you, I'm afraid, Hilary.'

'Nonsense.' Hilary gave Catrin a very straight look. 'And even if he does, Catrin, perhaps you might get it across to him that men who belong to other ladies are out of bounds as far as I'm concerned.'

The other girl nodded soberly. 'I've told him that. I'll tell him again, too. Don't worry. Come downstairs and share a great big pizza I brought home from Newport. No Rhys tonight, I promise.'

Hilary hadn't the heart to refuse a second time, and passed a very pleasant evening, eventually pleading weariness and the need for an early night. As she unlocked her door the phone began to ring. She banged the door shut and ran to answer it.

'I've been ringing you most of the evening,' said Rhodri's deep voice, the musical lilt in it lifting each separate little hair along Hilary's spine.

'Who is this?' she said, brusque in her effort to sound calm.

'You know who it is, Hilary Mason. Don't try to box clever.' Rhodri laughed softly. 'I said I'd ring, so I'm ringing. Are you well?'

'Very well. Are you?'

'A trifle weary after a hectic day, but all the better for hearing your voice—at last.'

'I've been having supper with Catrin Probert in the flat below——'

'And did her brother come too?' he said swiftly.

'No.'

'Good.' There was a pause. 'What are you doing this weekend?'

Hilary thought fast. Now was the time to nip all this in the bud. 'I'm going away,' she lied, crossing her fingers.

'That's a pity. I'll be in your part of the world. I was hoping you might be free for dinner on Saturday, or lunch on Sunday.'

'What a shame.' Hilary closed her eyes and steeled herself. 'I'm not likely to be back until late Sunday evening.'

'That's a blow. I'm disappointed.' Rhodri paused, then his voice deepened. 'Are *you* disappointed too, Hilary?'

'Of course,' she said lightly. 'A free meal is always an attractive prospect.'

He was silent so long that Hilary thought he'd rung off. 'You know how to cut a man down to size,' said Rhodri at last. 'There I was, haunted by the memory of those blue eyes of yours all day, when all the time you were probably thinking about the salmon, not me.'

Hilary felt stricken, but took a grip on herself. 'Oh, no,' she assured him gaily. 'Both the salmon *and* you, I promise.'

'A crumb of comfort, I suppose. I'll give you a ring some other time, perhaps.'

'Lovely. Thank you so much for ringing. Goodnight.'

And Hilary replaced the receiver, rolled over face down on her bed and shed a few bitter tears into her pillow.

Fool! she told herself fiercely. Why hadn't she just said yes, as she wanted to? Did it really matter if the man's blood was bluer than hers? As Candida said, no one gave a hoot about that sort of thing these days. And even if Rhodri's intentions weren't likely to be of a permanent kind, would it have been so terrible to indulge in a love-affair with him?

Yes, came the answer. Because after Rhodri no other man was likely to stand up to comparison. Ever. There was no point in wrecking her life in the long term for the sake of a little will-power right now, before she reached the point where she was likely to consent to anything Rhodri Lloyd-Ellis cared to ask. And it might be as well to remember that not so long ago he'd been all set to marry someone else, and was probably still hankering after the lady in question.

Fortified by these sensible arguments, Hilary did her best to put Rhodri from her mind as she threw herself into life at the library by day, and set herself to work her way through the complete works of Jane Austen at night, with the addition of a modern thriller or romance thrown in now and then by way of contrast. She wrote long letters to her parents, extolling the attractions of Penafon, and her satisfaction with her job, saw quite a bit of Catrin, and one evening enjoyed a meal in the Hughes household, where Olwen and her husband Gwyn, plus two lively teenage sons and a couple of dogs, were very hospitable company.

When the weekend arrived Hilary refused to think of the evening she might have spent with Rhodri, and listened to the Saturday play on the radio, then read until her eyes swam and she was tired enough to sleep. Sunday was long. It was too wet to go out for a walk, and after attending Matins at the church she concocted a high-fibre, low-calorie lunch, did some ironing, and made calculations to see how much money she could put aside out of her salary to save for a television. Catrin was staying the weekend with her parents in Caerleon, and without her neighbour's lively company for coffee and a chat now and then the time dragged intolerably. It hadn't before Rhodri's advent, Hilary reminded herself, therefore she must learn not to let it do so in future.

Nevertheless, when a knock sounded on her door in the middle of the evening, Hilary sprang eagerly to open it, hoping Catrin had come back. Her smile of welcome faded as she saw Rhys Probert instead, leaning against the balcony rail, looking amused at the suspicion on Hilary's face.

'Hello, Rhys. Catrin's with your parents,' she said.

'I know.' He pushed himself upright. 'That's why I'm here. I thought you might be glad of a little company. Won't you ask me in?'

'Not on your life! I value my reputation too much to entertain a man alone in my flat.'

'Who would know?'

'The whole town, probably. Within minutes.'

He laughed. 'Then come out with me and have a drink.'

'No, thanks, Rhys. Not tonight. I—I have to wash my hair,' she improvised hastily.

'Oh, come on! One drink won't hurt you.' Suddenly the breadth of Rhys's rugby-forward shoulders looked menacing. 'Because if you won't come out I'll come in. Or are you choosy as to what company you keep? Perhaps I don't compare with Lloyd-Ellis?'

'If you'll wait in the car I'll be down in five minutes,' said Hilary, deciding to placate him. 'I need to tidy myself up.'

He eyed her challengingly. 'All right, *cariad*. Five minutes—or I'll be up to get you.'

Hilary could well believe it, and hurried over her hair and face, deciding her cord jeans and fisherman's jersey would have to do. She threw on her trenchcoat and locked her door, then ran downstairs to the waiting black shape of Rhys's car.

'Right,' she said tartly, as she climbed in. 'I've kept my promise, now you keep yours. One drink—and *not* at the Afon Arms because I'm not dressed for it. Let's go to the White Lion. I go in there for a sandwich at lunch sometimes, and it's rather nice.'

'Whatever you say,' said Rhys, and within minutes they were seated in the lounge bar of the little pub near the library, Hilary with a glass of lager and her companion with a double whisky.

'Where's Lynne tonight?' asked Hilary deliberately, and Rhys scowled at her.

'No need to worry about Lynne.'

'But I do. Doesn't she mind when you take other women out?'

'She—puts up with it,' he said morosely, and looked at her from under heavy black brows. 'Let's not talk about her.'

'Right. We'll change the subject.' Hilary looked him in the eye. 'This is a one-off, Rhys. Just to put you in the picture as far as I'm concerned. I'm not in the market for a little dalliance with a man who is morally, if not legally, bound to someone else. In fact, dalliance with anyone isn't my type of thing.'

'Not even Lloyd-Ellis?'

'No,' she said coldly. 'Not that it's any concern of yours.'

'If I told Lynne it was over between us, would it make any difference to you?' he asked, after an uncomfortable silence.

Hilary glared at him. 'No, it wouldn't. Not that the question arises, because I happen to know from Catrin that Lynne is the daughter of your senior partner. You've no intention of endangering your position in the firm, have you?'

'Catrin's a sight too free with her information.' He reached for the empty glass. 'Let me get you another drink.'

'No, thanks.' Hilary stood up decisively. 'One drink we agreed on, and now I'm going home. If you don't want to drive me I can easily walk.'

Rhys sighed, and got to his feet. 'OK, OK, Hilary. I'll take you home.'

The whole episode had taken less than an hour from the time Hilary locked her door until the time she opened it again, but it seemed like four times as long. She turned to Rhys with such open relief to be back home that his face darkened as she smiled at him.

'Goodnight, Rhys. Thank you for the drink.' Before she had realised his intention he lifted her up by the elbows and thrust her through her own front door, kicking it shut behind him.

'Not so fast,' he growled, and yanked her into his arms.

By this time Hilary was very fed up with Rhys Probert, and blazingly angry. Avoiding his descending mouth, she hit out at him as she knew she should have done the first time he kissed her. Her father had taught her when she was quite young always to use a clenched fist, and the fury behind her blow lent added strength, catching Rhys squarely on his large nose, and surprising him so much he released her instantly to clap a hand to the injured feature, as blood streamed from it down his face.

'What the hell do you think you're doing?' he howled, hunting for a handkerchief, and Hilary went into her minuscule bathroom for a handful of tissues and handed them over.

'Here,' she said tersely. 'Now go.'

Suddenly a loud knock on the door made them both jump.

'Bloody hell,' swore Rhys. 'I bet that's Catrin.'

It wasn't. When Hilary opened the door she stared up in dismay at the last person in the world she wanted to see at that particular moment. Rhodri Lloyd-Ellis stood staring straight past her at Rhys Probert's bloodstained face. He held an envelope in his hand, and his face was grim and cold. No laughter-lines tonight, she saw with foreboding.

'Forgive me if I intrude,' he said with frosted courtesy. 'I was passing and thought I'd push a note through your door, since you were away.'

'Rhodri—hello, what a surprise,' stammered Hilary, and glowered at Rhys. 'Let me introduce you to Rhys Probert, my neighbour's brother. He's just going.'

Rhodri nodded at the discomfited Rhys. 'Lloyd-Ellis,' he said, looking down his nose at the shorter man in a way that made Hilary's heart sink. Since he wasn't granted the favour of a hand to shake Rhys was obliged to nod in acknowledgement, finding himself with no alternative to removing himself, however reluctantly.

'Hello,' he said indistinctly, and was forced to sniff inelegantly, as blood continued to stream from his nose.

'You need a cold compress on that,' Rhodri advised him, and Rhys scowled as he turned to Hilary.

'Goodnight, Hilary. Thanks a lot.' He looked up at the taller man with a slight smile. 'But I think you got your wires crossed somewhere, Lloyd-Ellis. She hasn't been away, she's been out with me.'

The silence he left behind him after he slammed the door would have pleased Rhys Probert immeasurably,

as Hilary looked up at her second visitor of the evening
with guilt in her eyes.

'Why the lies, Hilary?' said Rhodri harshly. 'If you
didn't want another evening with me all you had to do
was say so. I've no right to object if you prefer Probert's
company to mine.'

Hilary went into her tiny kitchen and filled the kettle.
'I don't. How do you imagine he came by his bloody
nose? He didn't walk into a door. I hit him.'

'With what, exactly?'

His voice was heavy with sarcasm, and Hilary threw
a hostile glance at him over her shoulder, angry with
herself because the mere sight of his tall frame lounging
in her kitchen doorway turned her fingers into thumbs
as she measured coffee into mugs and poured boiling
water, searching blindly for sugar and milk. 'My fist,'
she said tightly, and waved it at him. The knuckles were
grazed and bleeding, and Rhodri took her hand in his,
staring down at it.

'What the hell was the man doing?' he demanded.

'He tried to kiss me.'

'Is that all?'

'Isn't it enough?' she said, incensed. 'I didn't want
him to kiss me, I didn't want him in my flat, and for
your information I didn't want to go out for a drink
with him, either, but he was so—so menacing, somehow,
earlier on, that I thought I'd be better off in a pub than
up here, if he forced his way in, as he said he would if
I didn't go out.'

Rhodri dropped her hand and made for the door,
flinging it open to lean over the landing rail to see if
there was a light in the flat below.

'He won't be there,' said Hilary, looking down into
the street. 'His car's gone.'

'Pity!' Rhodri came back in and shut the door, then took the coffee she handed him. 'I think it's time Mr Probert learned a lesson about molesting defenceless women.' Then suddenly he grinned, and to Hilary it was like the sun coming out after the storm. 'Not that I could describe you as defenceless, exactly. On two of the four occasions I've been in your company you've just finished trouncing two males almost twice your fighting weight!'

Hilary's answering smile was brilliant with relief. She gestured towards her sofa, and curled up at one end of it while Rhodri sat down at the other, half-turned towards her. 'So much for my precious reputation,' she said ruefully. 'In spite of effort from both you and me I've had not one but *two* men under my roof tonight, and the church clock hasn't struck nine yet.'

'I suppose I shouldn't be here.' Rhodri drank some of his coffee, his eyes meeting hers. 'But after all that fracas I didn't fancy leaving you alone.'

Hilary looked away. 'Normally I'm as safe here as I'm likely to be anywhere. I was stupid enough to open my door to Rhys because I thought he was someone else.'

Rhodri abandoned his coffee and moved along the sofa to take her hand. 'Did you by any chance think it would be me?'

Colour rose in Hilary's cheeks. 'No. It never occurred to me. I thought it was Catrin.'

He winced and grinned at her, the warmth from his body reaching hers and making her tremble. 'How you do deflate my ego, Hilary!'

'I don't mean to.' At such close range she could see the fine texture of his skin, and how crystal-clear the whites of his eyes gleamed against the dark-rimmed grey irises, and the darker fringe of enviably thick lashes. He had taken off his suede jerkin, and wore a grey cashmere sweater over a cream wool shirt, the elegant length of his legs even more pronounced than usual in dark blue cords a little rubbed at the knee. As he leaned even closer Hilary became conscious of the clean, male scent of him, and swallowed nervously.

'What is it?' he asked softly.

'I—I was wondering what you were actually doing here in Penafon tonight.'

'I came on the off chance to see if you'd returned from your weekend and, if not, to deliver a note, in case some local citizen had seen a stranger lurking near your flat.' He stayed where he was, as close to her as was possible without actually crowding her, and since Hilary was restricted by the arm of the sofa there was nowhere she could retreat without actually getting up. And she didn't want to get up. She wanted to stay where she was, just like this, indefinitely.

'Are you going to give me the note?' she whispered, mesmerised by the gleaming grey eyes so close to her own.

'Since it was merely a substitute for what I really wanted, I haven't decided yet.' He raised her grazed knuckles to his mouth and kissed them gently, still holding her eyes with his. 'Hilary—would I be utterly mistaken in thinking that perhaps you wouldn't resort to violence if *I* kissed you?'

Hilary shook her head, then closed her eyes sharply as Rhodri took her in his arms and kissed her mouth with a tenderness that shook her to the depths of her being. She leaned into him, all her bones suddenly liquid at the touch of his lips on hers, and with an inarticulate murmur Rhodri drew her on to his lap and tightened his arms about her, his mouth abruptly urgent. How strange, she thought, while she was still capable of thought, that kisses one yearned for were so different from kisses one feared. But after only a moment or two Hilary gave up thinking without a struggle, lost to everything other than the hard, warm mouth wooing hers with such unimagined skill and delicacy. She wriggled closer instinctively, their united warmth, even through the layers of clothing, suddenly igniting to a degree where she felt bathed in fire as her mouth opened with a gasp of delight.

Rhodri muttered indistinctly against her open lips, and a great tremor ran through his body as he pressed her head against his shoulder and laid his cheek against her hair. Hilary shivered in response, and with a groan he put a finger under her chin and raised her willing mouth to his. She could feel the tension in his spare, elegant body, the long, flat athlete's muscles taut beneath her questing fingers as she ran them tentatively over his back. His kiss deepened, his tongue, restrained at first, bolder as it recognised its welcome. They breathed in unison, raggedly and unevenly, and a long-fingered hand slid beneath her jersey, seeking out the generous curves beneath it. As his fingertips sought the hard, quivering tips of her breasts through the thin barrier of lace, Hilary gave a shuddering cry and burrowed against him, then pulled away, shaking her head as she turned her face away, her eyes closed against the heated question in his.

What was she *doing*! It was exactly what she'd been afraid of. Not only Rhodri's expectations but her own response to them. With supreme reluctance she opened eyes she knew quite well were heavy with the feeling dammed inside her.

Rhodri reached out an unsteady hand and touched her hot cheek. 'I frightened you.' The light in his glittering eyes was almost blinding. 'Don't be frightened, Hilary. I won't hurt you.'

'Oh, but you will, you will,' she said, in a low, shaking voice.

'How can you say that?'

'How can you avoid it?' She jumped to her feet. 'I said earlier tonight, to another man entirely, that I am not in the market for dalliance——'

Rhodri sprang up, looking thunderstruck, his eyes narrowed as he glared down at her. '*Dalliance!* What the hell do you mean by that?'

'Exactly what I say. I'm not available for—for that sort of thing.'

'Hilary, I think you read too many books!'

She rounded on him. 'Possibly. But there's nothing fictional about the fact that—that you wanted to make love to me just now.'

He raised an arrogant eyebrow. 'I thought I *was* making love to you.'

'You know what I mean,' she said impatiently. 'Bed, and all that.'

'Ah! Bed and all that. I see.'

'I don't think you do. For you I imagine it's nothing out of the ordinary——'

'Do you really?'

'Oh, please,' said Hilary in desperation. 'I'm doing my best to explain.'

'Try harder.'

She sighed, staring up at him fixedly. 'I've found out your grandfather was an earl.'

Rhodri's face went utterly blank. 'So?'

'I didn't know.'

'There was no reason why you should!'

'No. But it makes a difference.'

'Why? He was Irish and stony broke, but a right old charmer—no insanity or anything like that.'

'Maybe not, but he was still an earl.'

'Is it possible you're a snob, Hilary? Do my relations have anything to do with my eligibility as a lover, for heaven's sake?'

'That's it,' she cried. 'You've said it. That's how you would think of any—anything between us. Lovers. But in my family the women don't have lovers.'

'Including Candida?' he demanded. 'Are you telling me that all the men who swarm after her are content with platonic relationships?'

'If not they get shown the door. They never get as far as her bed.'

Rhodri sat down suddenly. 'I haven't asked to be your lover, Hilary.'

'No,' she agreed. 'It was blindingly obvious just now that you don't need to. I was humiliatingly ready—oh, please, Rhodri,' she said, flinging away blindly. 'You know exactly what I'm getting at.'

'I'm not sure,' he said slowly. 'You don't want me as a lover, I gather, though it's fairly conclusive that we'd be highly compatible. Do I take it you'd be more receptive to the idea of me as a husband?'

Hilary whirled round, aghast. 'Lord, no! Not in the least. People like you don't marry people like me. And even if you weren't the grandson of an earl and all that, you'd still be highly ineligible as far as I'm concerned. I happened to hear, from an unimpeachable source, that it isn't so very long since you badly wanted to marry a lady—presumably in your own social bracket—who had the bad taste to prefer someone else.'

'Do go on,' he said, in a flat tone.

Hilary looked down at him bleakly. 'It's quite simple really. Apart from the obvious social barrier between us, Rhodri, I just don't fancy any type of relationship with a man who'd look on me as second best—as a sort of consolation prize.'

Rhodri rose to his not inconsiderable height, and looked down his nose at her rather in the way he had at Rhys Probert earlier. 'Just for the record,' he said at last, 'the lady in question is the daughter of the rector in the village of Cwmderwen where we both grew up. And the reason Sarah turned me down was nothing to do with any arcane social differences. She just happened to be irrevocably in love with another man.'

Hilary looked up into his closed face, unable to bring herself to ask whether he still loved the unknown Sarah. 'Was she pretty?' she asked inanely, and raged at herself silently, as Rhodri smiled with infuriating indulgence.

'Yes. Very.' He touched a hand to her untidy hair. 'Quite beautiful in fact, if you want the truth.'

Hilary found the truth depressingly unpalatable, and looked pointedly at her watch. 'It's late. I don't want to be rude, but I think it's time you went.'

He put an ungentle hand under her chin and turned her face up to his. She flushed angrily, and he shook his head in reproof. 'Don't even think about using your fist, young lady. Now listen to me. Sarah, like Candida, is a portrait painted in vivid, primary colours. You, on the other hand, possess a subtle, haunting quality—like a watercolour.'

'Insipid, you mean,' said Hilary, and freed herself.

'No, I don't,' he retorted, shrugging into his jerkin. 'But, as you say, it's late, and I don't think I'd get anywhere if I stayed to try and persuade you differently.'

An envelope fell from his pocket, and Hilary bent to pick it up to return it to him, her teeth catching on her lower lip as she saw her own name written on the envelope. Rhodri took it away from her.

'No point in your reading that now,' he said quickly. 'Your little homily just now rendered the contents irrelevant.'

Wild with curiosity, Hilary was forced to exert considerable self-control not to beg to read the note, since it was plain Rhodri had no intention of handing it over.

'I'd better be off, then,' Rhodri said briskly, and went to the door. 'Don't come outside, Hilary. I'll wait to hear you lock the door after me, then I'll take myself off to Oxford and the loneliness of my empty house.'

'I wouldn't have thought a man like you was lonely very often,' remarked Hilary.

'A man like me,' he repeated drily. 'What kind of man do you think that is, I wonder? One who goes round seducing young, innocent girls, from the sound of it, not to mention lusting after another man's wife at one and the same time.'

'I didn't say *that*,' she said despairingly. 'I—I just wanted——'

'Hilary,' he interrupted abruptly. 'Just exactly how old *are* you?'

She hesitated, then thought better of adding on a year or two. 'Twenty,' she said reluctantly.

'Is that all!' Colour flared unexpectedly along Rhodri's cheekbones, then receded as Hilary watched, depressed. 'I had no idea you were as young as that. When Candida said you were qualified I naturally assumed you were well into your twenties.'

'I was rather a bright child,' she informed him expressionlessly. 'I passed all my exams early, went off to college early, and got my qualifications right on cue.'

He nodded slowly. 'But in spite of all that you're still not really much more than a child in some ways.' He smiled ruefully. 'I think I'd better leave you to get on with your growing-up, Hilary—you've rather more of it to do than I'd realised.'

'Goodbye then,' said Hilary stonily. 'I'm sorry you came such a long way out of your way for nothing.'

Rhodri bent swiftly and kissed her mouth with an abrupt force that was over before she had time to protest. 'Not entirely for nothing, Hilary,' he said roughly, then opened the door and gave her an odd, mocking salute before he closed it quietly behind him.

Her teeth sunk deep into her lower lip, Hilary shot the bolts and slid in the safety chain, listening to Rhodri's footsteps ringing on the iron stair, then she leaned her forehead against the door, staying where she was long after the sound of the convertible's quiet engine was only a memory in the cold Sunday quiet of the night.

CHAPTER SIX

HER love-affair with the world of fiction had always been Hilary's emergency exit from the real world when the going got rough. But in the period which followed the events of that singularly testing Sunday evening her escape route stayed obstinately blocked. She could lose herself neither in the latest additions to the library's shelves, nor in the old favourites which stood in neatly stacked piles by her bed, at the end of the kitchen counter, on the shelves in her sitting-room and bathroom and on any other surface which offered sufficient space.

Hilary's entry into the library school attached to Birmingham University, as she had told Rhodri, had been achieved very young, and during her time there various boyfriends had come and gone but none of them had ever really shaken her from her belief that the written word held far greater fascination than any of the spoken importunities she had listened to over the years from members of the opposite sex.

It had come as a great surprise to Hilary to find that a few brief moments in Rhodri Lloyd-Ellis's arms beat any love-passages she had ever read, from Shakespeare, Brontë and Flaubert right up to, and including, various modern purveyors of romantic fiction. Reading about it was no substitute at all for the experience itself.

Since those few short minutes looked like being all she was likely to have now Rhodri knew how old she was, or, more to the point, was *not*, Hilary decided the best way to forget them was to occupy herself in other ways, to which end she presented herself at Cwmderwen Court

Hotel a few days later, with a view to finding extra work. The fact that it had once belonged to Rhodri Lloyd-Ellis was entirely incidental, she assured herself, but felt depressed none the less by the austere eighteenth-century beauty of the house she found at the end of a long drive. This, she reminded herself sternly, had been his childhood home. It was in this parkland that the young Rhodri had been privileged to run free, on an estate not only large enough to contain a stretch of fishing rights on the Wye, but to allow for the creation of a nine-hole golf course when the house was eventually converted into a hotel.

Hilary parked her Mini discreetly away from the house, then went inside to keep the appointment she had made over the phone with the manageress. She found herself in a small, but beautifully proportioned entrance hall, with only a rosewood escritoire as reception desk to hint that this was a hotel rather than a private house. Miss Lawson, a tall, cool blonde with an enviable figure and no-nonsense manner, was waiting in her office at the rear when the pleasant receptionist showed Hilary in, and was swift to establish what hours Hilary would be prepared to work, and whether she would stay overnight if necessary on Saturdays to help with Sunday breakfasts and to change beds after departing weekend guests.

It was soon agreed that Hilary would come straight to the hotel on Saturday afternoons when she finished at the library, and stay until nine on Mondays, which would give her half an hour to get back to the library again after helping with breakfasts, or any other task necessary in the time allotted.

'Are you sure you wish to give up your spare time like this?' asked Erica Lawson. 'You're a little young to have no social life.'

'I could do with the money,' said Hilary frankly. 'And I'm used to dealing with the public, so it seems like the ideal arrangement if you think I'll suit.'

'I see. Very well. I'll expect you on Saturday next, in time to help with afternoon tea.'

Catrin was so disparaging about the extra job that Hilary decided not to tell Candida at all. If a friend of Catrin's short acquaintance was so obviously worried about the overwork and exhaustion predicted with such gloom and doom, Hilary decided to skip the storm of scolding she knew would break over her head once Candida realised what her little sister had in mind.

For the first couple of weekends Hilary wondered if she'd bitten off more than she could chew, as she learnt the complexities of serving afternoon tea, helping lay the tables for dinner, waiting on table during the meal, then re-laying the tables afterwards ready for breakfast the following morning.

She fell asleep as soon as her head touched the pillow in the tiny attic bedroom allotted to her, too tired to wonder if Rhodri had once played up here as a child, or even which room he'd actually occupied. And next morning she was up with the rest of the live-in staff, to prepare trays of morning tea and coffee, and deliver them to the various rooms before getting ready to serve breakfast.

Megan Hughes, a young relative of Olwen's husband Gwyn, was a great help in easing Hilary into the hotel's routine, checking on the readiness of toast-racks, teapots, coffee-pots, marmalade, preserves, then the serving of the meal itself—smiling—and the clearing away afterwards. Sunday lunch, mercifully, was not served in Cwmderwen Court Hotel. Once re-laid, the tables were ready for dinner in the evening, as Hilary found to her relief when she learnt the complexities of cleaning the rooms once weekend guests had checked out.

At first she thought she'd never get through it all, but after a while the tasks became automatic as she changed linen, replenished supplies of soap, headed notepaper, and unforeseen details like bin-liners, before going on to clean bathrooms and bedrooms. After staff lunch there was time for a short rest, and then it was all hands on deck for afternoon tea and the routine had come full circle.

'Money isn't everything, *cariad*,' said Olwen, as she eyed Hilary's haggard face the first Monday morning after the weekend stint at the hotel. 'Have some more of my Welsh-cakes, for goodness' sake.'

'I've got all week to recover,' said Hilary cheerfully, and kept her real reason for extra work to herself. The money was important enough, of course, but her main object was to fill the long, lonely weekends now there was no likelihood of further visits from Rhodri.

As expected, Hilary heard no more from him, but received a very welcome surprise a day or two later in the shape of money from her parents. 'Candida said you need a portable television,' wrote her mother. 'So sorry, darling, your father and I never gave it a thought—please buy yourself one with the enclosed.'

Hilary did so at once, thrilled by her gift, after which her evenings went by quite happily once she had a choice of screen, radio or literature, according to mood. Easter came quickly, with a few days off from the library. Hilary spent them all at the hotel, where the season was hotting up. The new bedroom extension had been constructed at top speed, and was due to open on Easter Monday. There was to be a reception for local townspeople in the evening, with a buffet supper, and because the hotel was also fully booked for the holiday it meant the entire staff would be working at full stretch, and Hilary agreed to sleep in for the whole holiday period.

Candida was very suspicious when Hilary turned down the offer of Easter in Oxford. 'What on earth are you going to do with yourself up there, then?' she demanded.

'I've been invited to stay with friends,' said Hilary. Which was more or less the truth. 'By the way,' she said quickly, changing the subject, 'Mother and Dad sent me money for a television. Thank you, big sister. I gather it was your doing.'

'I'd have liked to buy you one myself,' said Candida, 'but frankly I've spent too much money on clothes lately. Horribly frivolous, but I feel I must compete with the women Jack's exposed to most of the time in London.'

'Did you enjoy his play? It got very good reviews.'

'Yes, love, I did. He took me to supper afterwards at Langan's, and people recognised him and speculated on who I was and it was wonderful.'

'You don't sound overjoyed.'

'I just wish he were someone more ordinary. Like me.'

'I know how you feel,' said Hilary with a sigh, then took several minutes to reassure her sister that all was well and no, Rhodri hadn't been to see her since, nor was he expected to do so in the foreseeable future.

'Oh, Hilly! What on earth did you say to frighten him off?' demanded Candida irritably.

'Nothing much. The subject of my age came up, that's all.'

Whereupon there was a lengthy pep-talk on not taking Rhodri's reaction too much to heart, on how there were other fish in the sea, and a great deal more sisterly advice before Hilary was allowed to ring off.

The buffet was to be a formal affair, and all the waitresses were provided with a smart black dress with oak trees embroidered on the collar.

'That's what Cwmderwen means, see,' said Megan. 'Valley of the oak. So Miss Lawson was told to get these done. Nothing so menial as aprons for us tonight.'

A few minutes before the appointed hour the girls were given a break to change and tidy themselves ready for the invasion of the town dignitaries and the cutting of the ceremonial ribbon tied across the entrance of the annexe. The hotel was very popular both in Cwmderwen village and in the town of Penafon, since it provided jobs for the inhabitants of the former and trade for the latter, and was a draw for tourists who were always discreetly pointed in the direction of the pretty riverside town and its shops.

Hilary brushed her springy hair as smoothly as possible into the tight pleat she adopted for waiting on table, using only an eyeliner and a touch of lipstick on her face, since Miss Lawson was not in favour of vivid make-up on the faces of her staff.

'Particularly the men,' giggled Megan, as the two girls went down the back stairs to the dining-room where the long buffet table waited, loaded with masterpieces of the combined art of the three chefs. One of Hilary's skills was a way with flowers, and Erica Lawson had seized on the chance to economise, letting her newest employee decorate the table with the seasonal charm of daffodils and narcissus and long trails of forsythia, instead of calling in a professional florist.

'Trouble is,' said Megan, 'you'll get landed with the job every weekend, now. Our Erica's always one to take advantage.'

'As long as she pays me extra I'll jump at it,' Hilary assured her, and craned her neck to look through the tall windows with their swagged curtains, as cars began to draw up on the gravel of the forecourt outside.

'Our Erica's in her oils tonight anyway,' hissed Megan, as the first of the guests arrived in the hall. 'I heard the owner's coming, so she'll be dancing attendance on him all night instead of breathing down our necks.'

There was no time for more conversation, since guests were already filtering into the dining-room, and with the ease of weeks of practice Hilary hefted a silver tray laden with glasses of wine, and began to circulate among the throng. Soon the room was warm and noisy with the sound of animated voices talking at the tops of their voices as the wine loosened tongues and brought ready laughter from a crowd of people all set to enjoy themselves enormously.

Hilary hurried to and fro, refilling glasses, offering canapés, and smiling, smiling, as she exchanged brief pleasantries with people she had come to know in the course of both her jobs. Another batch of people surged into the room, and Hilary seized another heavily laden tray and advanced towards them to offer drinks, her smile suddenly fixed as she met a pair of astounded eyes, glittering like ice as they stared down into hers.

Rhodri Lloyd-Ellis here! thought Hilary in desperation, and widened her smile and went on proffering glasses of wine. Erica Lawson, in a black lace sheath far removed from her normal severe suit, had her hand in the crook of Rhodri's arm as she manoeuvred him from group to group, introducing him to strangers and renewing his acquaintance with people he already knew.

'He's arrived, then,' muttered Megan in an undertone, as they met briefly to collect a new supply of canapés.

'Who?' said Hilary.

'Rhodri Lloyd-Ellis, the owner. Proper dreamboat, isn't he?' sighed the other girl, and hurried off on her rounds.

Hilary decided that either she'd misheard Megan in the hubbub, or the other girl had her facts all wrong, and a few minutes later she took up her stance behind a superb salmon afloat on a sea of aspic, ready to serve portions as instructed. The three chefs, in full panoply of white, their tall hats towering, wielded carving knives with panache as they presided over the various superb cold roasts, while Hilary, now wearing an organdie apron over the smart black dress, served portions of the salmon with care, and smiled and smiled, and parried endless amused comments from frequenters of the library on her change of job.

After a while Megan sidled up and whispered, 'Miss Lawson wants to see you in the office. I'll take over here.'

Wondering if she'd done something wrong, Hilary knocked on the office door and went in, then stopped dead on the threshold. Rhodri was perched on a corner of the desk, but otherwise the room was empty.

'You? I thought Miss Lawson wanted me,' said Hilary.

'Hello, Hilary.' He slid off the desk and reached behind her to close the door, startling her by turning the key in the lock.

'You can't do that!' she said in trepidation. 'I'll lose my job——'

'Erica Lawson thinks I'm having a chat with the newest member of staff. No one will come. And even if they do it's of no consequence.' He smiled. 'It's my hotel.'

Hilary stared at him, her heart sinking at his words even as her eyes drank in the mere sight of him. She had seen Rhodri so few times, yet each time he was dressed with daunting elegance, even in casual sweater and cords, as on the last unforgettable occasion. Tonight he was something else. He wore a suit in such ultrafine checks of black and white that it looked plain light grey at first glance. His shirt gleamed white and pristine in contrast to the sober, dark-grey silk of his tie, and his long, narrow feet were shod in handstitched black calf.

'Will I do?' he asked drily.

Hilary looked away, discomfited. 'Why did you send for me?'

'I wanted to know what the hell you're playing at?' he demanded fiercely. 'Why have you left your job at the library to do—*this*?'

A long finger flicked at her apron, and Hilary backed away.

'I haven't left the library. I work here in my spare time.'

His eyebrows met over incredulous grey eyes. 'You mean you do this on *top* of your other job?'

She nodded defiantly.

'Why, for Pete's sake?'

'The usual reason,' she said, lifting her chin. 'Money. I need it.'

He sat on the edge of the desk again, stretching out his long legs. 'What for?'

'I believe that's my business.'

'If you work in an establishment belonging to me I consider certain things about my staff *are* my business. And one of them is their physical welfare. You look bloody awful, Hilary.'

'It's the dress,' she muttered, flushing. 'I look hideous in black.'

'I doubt very much you could look hideous in anything.' Rhodri looked her up and down assessingly. 'Though now you come to mention it I'd be very happy if you took that blasted dress off.'

'Now?' she asked cuttingly.

His smile flustered her. 'Why, yes—if you wish.'

Hilary glanced nervously towards the door. 'I must get back—I'll be missed.'

'Since you're known to be here with me, no one will remark on it.'

She snorted. 'Oh, yes, they will!'

'Not to me, I assure you,' he said suavely.

'Well, they will to me. And I have to work with the others in future, so please let me go now.'

'Not until you tell me why you need money so badly.' He went over to the door and leaned his shoulders against it comfortably.

Hilary sighed in exasperation. 'You really don't have any idea about people like me, do you? You're so busy wheeling and dealing in your ivory tower of a City bank, with your house and your hotel and your gorgeous car, that you just don't relate to someone who does the job she wants to because it's the one she likes above all others. Which doesn't mean the pay's good, Mr Lloyd-Ellis. So if I want to keep my little flat, which I love, and run my old banger of a car, and pay my bills and eat, then I need a little extra. I don't want fur coats and diamonds and riotous living. Just security. It's as simple as that.'

Rhodri looked down at her, rubbing his chin. 'All right,' he said crisply. 'It's obvious we can't talk any longer here. I'll come and see you tonight at the flat.'

'Sorry. I'm sleeping here at the hotel, once I've finished work for the day. I share a room with Megan,' she added deliberately.

His jaw tightened. 'When *do* you finish here?'

'Tomorrow morning, after I've helped with the breakfast and done my share of the rooms.'

Rhodri made no comment. He unlocked the door and held it open for her. 'I suppose we'd both, in our various guises, better return to the fray.'

Hilary escaped with relief, in time to collect the dirty plates. In the swift, practised routine of clearing up there

was no time to talk with any of the others, though she
was burningly aware of the curiosity on the amused faces
of the rest of the staff. Erica Lawson was in evidence
only once, to check that everything was going smoothly,
but her glacial blue eyes alighted on Hilary's face with
a look that boded ill for the newest part-time member
of staff.

When, at last, she was free to climb the stairs on
throbbing feet to bed, Hilary was resigned to a barrage
of questions from Megan, but parried them with the information that Mr Lloyd-Ellis had merely wished to in-
terview the new employee personally.

'Pull the other one!' said Megan. 'You already know
each other, so I've heard.'

'Only slightly,' yawned Hilary. 'And I had no idea he
was the owner. I thought he sold the place ages ago.'
Otherwise she would never have set foot in Cwmderwen
Court Hotel, she thought passionately.

Their alarm shocked both girls into a mere groaning
semblance of life next morning, and both of them went
through the motions of preparing early-morning trays
like robots. Hilary's smile was an enormous effort as she
served breakfast, her stomach curling at the smell of
bacon and sausages, even kippers, worse still. Rhodri
breakfasted with Erica Lawson, but to Hilary's relief
their table was not among those allotted to her. Even so,
she was aware of his eyes following her as she hurried
to and fro with trays. It seemed an age before the dining-
room could be cleared and made ready for the evening
meal, leaving her free to collect her supply of linen and
cleaning materials to deal with the rooms vacated later
in the morning.

Hilary was just finishing the first of the bedrooms on
her rota when Erica Lawson swept in, her eyes piercing
as they roamed like lasers over the spotless room.

'When you've finished here you can go home,' she said crisply.

'But I've another three rooms to go——' began Hilary in surprise.

'Someone else will finish for you. Mr Lloyd-Ellis has instructed me to pay you the full amount and to inform you we are no longer in need of your services, since only full-time staff are required now the new extension is open.'

'Is my work unsatisfactory?' asked Hilary, dismayed.

'No, not in the least. You've worked very well.' The manageress shrugged. 'Your dismissal is not my idea, Hilary. It's Mr Lloyd-Ellis's directive. Come to the office when you're ready to leave.'

Hilary could hardly contain her rage as she took her supplies back to the store-room. She called in on Megan, who was busy a few doors along the hall, and told her what had happened.

'I thought something was up when you were called to the office last night,' the girl said. 'I noticed Mr Lloyd-Ellis's face when he first caught sight of you. If you ask me, he was livid.'

In stony silence Hilary collected the envelope containing her wages from Erica Lawson, her anger like a hot, red knot in her throat which made it difficult even to thank the manageress for the money. Of Rhodri there was no sign. Just as well, thought Hilary viciously, as she tried to start the Mini. Nothing happened. Hilary tried again, but there was no response at all.

Hilary could have screamed. It seemed the last straw. There was nothing for it but to walk down the mile-long drive and wait for a bus into Penafon. Which could prove a lengthy process. Hilary's knowledge of local transport was hazy, except that it was infrequent. But wait she must. Her sore feet throbbed even more at the prospect of a five-mile hike before she could kick her shoes off in the haven of her own flat.

Hilary had covered most of the distance to the main road when she caught sight of a familiar car parked under a group of the oaks which gave the house its name. The day was quite warm and sunny, and the Jaguar's hood was down, giving her a view of the unmistakable gleam of Rhodri's hair. She felt incandescent with the rage boiling inside her as she drew nearer to the car, knowing full well he was watching her in the car mirror even though his back was turned. As she drew level with the long, gleaming car he leaned over and opened the door on the passenger side.

'Get in, Hilary,' he ordered.

She had loosened her hair from its pleat once she left the hotel, and she pushed a hand through it angrily, glaring at him. 'I'd rather walk,' she spat, and passed him, her chin in the air.

He started the car, and drove at a crawl beside her. 'It's a good five miles.'

'Perhaps I'll get lucky and hitch a lift.'

'You've got a lift.'

'I told you. I'd rather walk.' Hilary marched on, her temper lending wings to her sore feet.

'Aren't you being rather unreasonable?' he said, smiling faintly.

'I think I'm damn well entitled to be!'

'That's what I want to talk about. Your job.'

'I have a job. I still work at the library.' She turned a fulminating blue glare on him. 'Unless, of course, you've managed to get me the sack there, too.'

'Now you're being childish.'

Hilary breathed in deeply, struggling to hold on to her temper. 'Please go away.'

Rhodri stopped the car and leapt out of it, striding towards Hilary with a look on his face she disliked intensely. Without arguing any further he scooped her up and dumped her in a sprawling heap in the passenger seat of the convertible, then sprang into the driver's seat and was off down the drive to the main gate before Hilary had regained her balance. 'Fasten your seatbelt,' he ordered, and accelerated out on to the road with such speed that she hurriedly obeyed, if only for the sake of self-preservation.

Suddenly Hilary realised they were going the wrong way. 'What do you think you're doing?' she said incensed. 'This isn't the way to Penafon.'

'I know. We're going somewhere quiet where we can talk, Hilary, so you may as well calm down and enjoy the ride.' Rhodri gave a wry, sidelong smile at her scarlet face. 'I rather think my car, if not its owner, merits your full approval, so why waste a sunny spring day by thinking out several methods of torture you'd like to inflict on my person, when all the charm of the Vale of Usk lies spread out before your beautiful blue eyes?'

CHAPTER SEVEN

HILARY subsided, glowering through the windscreen in silence. From the corner of her eye she saw Rhodri glance at her once or twice, but she ignored him, keeping her eyes very pointedly on the road. Not that he wasn't good to look at, she conceded grudgingly, with his hair flying in the breeze. As usual he looked irritatingly wonderful, even in old denims and a sweater that was by no means new, very much like the clothes she herself was wearing. Not that *she* felt elegant. Far from it. Hilary was all too conscious of her untidy hair and a face not only bare of make-up, but pink of nose from exposure to the elements as the car sped, hood down, along a road unusually busy with holiday traffic.

'Aren't you going to ask me where we're going?' enquired Rhodri eventually.

Hilary continued to ignore him, staring steadfastly at the passing scenery.

'Do I take it you don't intend talking to me at all?' he added, with a smile she could see even from the corner of her eye. It added fuel to the blaze inside her, and Hilary bit back the retort she burned to make, pretending complete absorption in the descent they were making down the side of a hill towards a valley which she took to be the Vale of Usk. It lay spread before them in a sunlit tapestry of greens and rusts and yellows stretched on a circular frame of sheltering hills, and in her pleasure at the sight Hilary almost forgot her anger—but not quite. She nursed it resentfully as Rhodri turned the car off on a narrower road and drove skilfully along dizzying steep bends which swooped between high hedges towards a farm. As they reached it Rhodri leaned on the horn and a smiling, weatherbeaten man called a greeting and unfastened a gate to let them through to a narrow track leading towards a glint of water.

'Thanks, Bryn,' called Rhodri to the farmer, and waved to a woman who appeared in the doorway of the farmhouse. A few minutes later he brought the car to halt in a small clearing near a stream.

'Why are we here?' asked Hilary, breaking her vow of silence.

'I used to come here to fish when I was a kid. In school holidays I spent a lot of time with Gareth Morgan, the rector's son——'

'Brother of the beauteous Sarah, I suppose,' said Hilary, then flushed to the roots of her hair as Rhodri regarded her thoughtfully.

'You remembered,' he commented. 'Clever child. Of course, Sarah was only a chubby little tot when I used to hang round the Rectory.'

'But she changed,' said Hilary drily.

'We all grow up in time,' said Rhodri gently, his eyes crystal bright with emphasis as they met hers.

'Which I suppose means I have a long way to go.' Hilary lifted her chin. 'You think I'm childish because I'm furious over being sacked.'

'No. Only to refuse to listen to me.'

'All right. So I'll listen.'

Rhodri jumped out of the car and took a wicker picnic-basket from the back of the car. 'While you listen you can eat.'

Hilary longed to say she wasn't hungry. But she was. And because the look in his eye told her quite plainly Rhodri knew she longed to refuse it, she accepted a smoked-salmon sandwich and prepared to hear him out.

'Why did you sack me?' she asked baldly.

'Because I don't want you to work at the Court.'

'Why not?'

Rhodri went on with his own sandwich for a moment or two before answering. 'There are several reasons, Hilary, but some of them would only incense you even more, so shall we say that if you're determined to make a drudge of yourself I'd rather you did it in some establishment other than mine.'

'I'm not a drudge! I'm merely working to get a little money together.'

'Surely there are easier ways than grafting day and night at two jobs, Hilary!'

'I'm sure there are. But if so, they aren't immediately apparent, still less available, in the vicinity of Penafon. Besides,' she added, 'I only work—or worked—at the hotel on weekends. I go to bed early every night in the week to compensate.'

'For Pete's sake, child——'

'Will you stop referring to me as a child!' she said, exasperated, and Rhodri turned in his seat to look at her with mockery in his eyes.

'To someone of my age sweet and twenty is very much a child, believe me.'

'Ah yes,' she said, her eyes darkening. 'You said I had some growing up to do. I'd forgotten.' Which was untrue. His words had stung. 'In which case,' she pointed out reasonably, 'I would have thought you'd look on my desire to work as a sign of maturity.'

Rhodri looked unconvinced. 'Does Candida know?'

'No.' Hilary gave him a straight look. 'And I'd be very grateful if you didn't mention it if you run into her, by the way.' She smiled bleakly. 'I think you owe it to me, since you're the one who's made sure there's nothing to tell her, anyway.'

'If you're trying to make me feel sorry for you, you're succeeding, Hilary,' he said, with a wry smile.

'Good,' she said shortly. 'Could I have one of those apples, please?'

Rhodri handed one over and watched her crunch into it. 'If,' he began slowly, 'I could put you in the way of extra work of a less exhausting nature, would you thaw towards me a little, Hilary?'

'It depends,' she said warily.

'On what?'

'What the work is, naturally!'

'I don't know yet. Until yesterday I had no idea you were in such desperate straits, so I can't promise anything off the top of my head.'

Hilary regarded him thoughtfully. 'I don't see what you *can* do. You work in London, live in Oxford——'

'I've a good many contacts right here, remember.' Rhodri filled two beakers from an insulated jug. 'I'll see what I can do.'

'Couldn't I go on working at the hotel until you do?'

'Definitely not. Drink some coffee.'

Hilary did as he said, her anger subsiding now she was no longer hungry. After all the excess emotion she felt sleepy. The copse of trees behind them shaded them from the breeze, and the sun was warm. She slid further down in her seat, listening idly to the soothing splash of the busy stream while Rhodri packed away their picnic. Her eyelids drooped, and she blinked, suddenly aware of late nights and early mornings, then a yawn overtook her and her eyelids became weighted. I'll just rest my eyes for a moment or two, she thought foggily, then stopped thinking altogether, and slid into a doze.

She woke with a start, utterly disorientated. Gradually she realised she was wrapped in a rug, and the hood of the convertible was now insulating her from the bright spring day. Only it wasn't bright any more. Hilary struggled upright, yawning, and found Rhodri watching her over the book he was reading.

'I'm sorry——' She looked at her watch in dismay. 'Good heavens—I've slept for hours.'

'You were quite obviously exhausted, Hilary,' he said austerely. 'No—don't push the rug away. It's quite cold now.'

Hilary shivered a little, as she realised he was right. She gave him an embarrassed look. 'I must have slept like the dead.'

He nodded. 'I was afraid I'd wake you when I put the hood up, but not a bit of it. The process involves coping with no fewer than eight pressure studs and six hook-and-loop attachments, but Sleeping Beauty went right on sleeping. I even chanced leaving you to go off and have a word with Bryn and Mary Thomas, but when I got back you were still sleeping like the dead.' He eyed her with severity. 'It's obvious you've been overdoing it, Hilary.'

'This weekend was much busier than normal,' she said defensively. 'It was Easter, and there was the opening of the new block——'

'I intended inviting you to that,' he said, and looked away. 'That was the envelope I had ready to deliver when I found you fighting off Probert.'

'What changed your mind?'

Rhodri's smile was cynical. 'My dear child, if you remember how we parted that night I'm surprised you find it necessary to ask.' He glared at her suddenly. 'Then I find you there anyway, in my own hotel, dashing about with bloody great trays of drinks!'

'Oh, please!' she said irritably. 'Don't let's start that again. Particularly when you've made jolly sure I won't be dashing about with any more. Or at least not at your hotel—and while we're on the subject I had no idea it *was* your hotel, believe me, or I'd never have asked to work there. Why didn't you tell me you still owned Cwmderwen Court?'

Rhodri shrugged. 'I didn't dare. Your opinion was pretty scathing about my house and my job as it was. It hardly seemed politic to mention I also owned a hotel. Not that it mattered, as it happened,' he added bitterly. 'You made your opinion of my attentions very clear.'

'That's not exactly accurate, is it?' she said hotly. 'I said I wasn't available for what you had in mind, that's all.'

'How did you know *what* I had in mind?' he asked silkily. 'I don't remember asking for anything in particular. We exchanged a few highly enjoyable kisses— enjoyable on my part, anyway. Then you read me a lecture on my brand of morality, as I remember it.'

Put like that it sounded very silly, and Hilary looked at him thoughtfully. 'In other words, I jumped the gun a bit. You didn't want to go to bed with me.'

Rhodri smiled slowly. 'Wrong. I did, believe me. But I didn't *expect* you to go to bed with me. There's a difference.'

Hilary could see the difference quite well, and was only sorry she hadn't been so clear-sighted at the time. 'I'm sorry,' she said stiffly. 'It seems I was a bit stupid about the whole thing.'

He reached out a hand and touched her cheek gently. 'Not stupid. Inexperienced, perhaps. Although I can't imagine I'm the first man to want to take you to bed, Hilary.'

'No, but you're the first I've——' She stopped short, swallowing. 'I mean, you're the first man I've ever allowed to reach the stage where it was even a consideration.'

'That's a very great compliment, Miss Mason. I'm honoured.' His slim forefinger touched her lower lip fleetingly, then fastened her seatbelt. 'How would you feel about spending an hour or two in the Thomases' kitchen at the farm, over a plate of home-cured bacon, and eggs fresh from the hens?'

Hilary's stomach gave an embarrassing rumble at the mere thought, and she apologised, giggling. 'Is that why you went to speak to them? To ask them to give us a meal?'

Rhodri nodded as he looked over his shoulder to reverse carefully for a few yards until he was able to turn on to the track. 'There's only one snag. The Thomases have gone out for the evening to visit one of their sons and his family, and you'd have to cook the food.'

'Well, really!' Hilary hooted. 'What a cheek, Rhodri Lloyd-Ellis!'

'You mean the bit about being alone at the farm, or the cooking?'

Hilary gave him a long, considering look. 'Only the latter. I don't imagine a man like you would fancy a repeat performance of our other evening together.'

'Which part of it?' asked Rhodri, grinning, as he stopped the car in the farmyard.

'You know quite well,' she said primly, then spoilt it by grinning back as he helped unwind her from her wool cocoon. 'I'm done up like a mummy,' she protested when she was free. 'I can't think how I didn't wake when you were wrapping me up like that.'

'You grunted a bit, that's all. Very ladylike little grunts,' he added as he took her hand to run the gauntlet of the two black and white collies who came to warn them off. 'All right, Nip—down, Bracken,' he said, as he quietened the barking dogs, who began frisking about him in welcome as they recognised him.

'You're obviously well known here,' commented Hilary, as they went into the big square kitchen, which was warm and welcoming, with a big scrubbed table and ladderback chairs, and a great Welsh dresser stacked with blue willow-pattern china against one wall. An Aga stove stood against another, giving out warmth Hilary deeply appreciated. 'Brr!' she said, leaning against it. 'This is lovely. Are you sure the Thomases don't mind us making free with their kitchen?'

'Quite sure. Mary's left us a note, so you can see for yourself.'

'Bacon and eggs in the larder,' their absent hostess had written. 'Tomatoes and mushrooms in the fridge. Help yourself to anything you fancy. PS: Apple tart in warming oven.'

One end of the table was laid with a spotless, embroidered cloth, set with heavy old silver and some of the willow-patterned plates. A crusty loaf stood on a wooden board alongside a dish of yellow butter and a hefty wedge of cheese, flanked by various jars of home-made pickle and relishes.

'Delicious,' said Hilary gleefully, and lifted the cover from the hottest plate on the stove, then slid a giant frying-pan into place over the heat. 'Right, then, Squire, you know the place so you raid the larder and I'll inspect the fridge.'

Rhodri pulled a lock of hair with mock servility, and went off to fetch several rashers of bacon and four eggs. 'I thought you couldn't cook, Miss Mason,' he commented when he came back, as he watched her rapidly trimming the rashers with kitchen scissors before arranging them on the sizzling pan.

'You want *boeuf en croûte* or something, I can't. Bacon and eggs I can. Put two dinner-plates in the oven, please.'

Amused, Rhodri did as he was bid, and professed his
deep admiration at the speed with which Hilary cooked
a meal they fell on ravenously, as though their picnic
lunch had never happened.

'Not much of the polyunsaturated about this,' he said,
mouth full, 'but marvellous just the same.'

'Better than the meal you had last night?' asked Hilary
slyly.

'Different. *And*,' he said with meaning, 'I'm enjoying
this much more. For very obvious reasons.'

Hilary helped herself to a spoonful of tomato chutney,
not looking at him. 'Which are?'

He shrugged. 'Let's say that last night the sight of you
waiting hand foot and finger on everyone in sight utterly
destroyed my appetite. Did you enjoy *your* dinner last
night?' he added, waving a fork at her.

'I didn't have any,' she confessed. 'I just fell into bed
after Megan made me a cup of cocoa last thing, and that
was that until dawn hit me in the face this morning.'

'Which only underlines the fact that you've been
overdoing it.'

And the fact that the mere sight of him had shocked
her so much, Hilary reflected secretly, that her normally
healthy appetite had vanished into thin air after one laser-
like glance from the grey eyes now watching her with
such suspicion.

'You haven't got some bee in your bonnet about
slimming, I hope?' he said, and pushed the cheese
towards her.

Hilary frowned. 'No. Do I need to?'

Rhodri looked her up and down dispassionately,
making her wish she was wearing something rather more
fetching than denims and one of her older jumpers.
'You're nicely rounded,' he said absently. 'Not as slender

as Candida, of course, but then I imagine she's the type who lives on carrot sticks and designer water.'

Candida was one of the fortunate mortals able to eat like a horse and never put on an inch, and Hilary was quick to tell Rhodri so, with a vehemence which made him smile.

'All right, all right,' said Rhodri, putting up his hands in surrender. 'I'll remember. No hint of criticism allowed about your exquisite sister or you reach for the nearest blunt instrument.'

'Right!' Hilary got up to take their plates. 'Want some of the tart Mrs Thomas mentioned?'

Both of them ate large portions of the delicious apple tart, accompanied by wedges of cheese, after which Hilary, protesting, was made to curl up on a comfortable leather sofa near the stove while Rhodri cleared away and washed up.

'Let me at least dry the dishes,' she said, feeling unhappy in the role of spectator.

'No chance. You've been working today. I haven't.' He shot her a teasing glance over his shoulder. 'And don't imagine this is likely to be a habit. Tonight's a one-off.'

Hilary watched him thoughtfully, wondering what he meant by a one-off. Was it the washing up he was referring to, or their evening together? At the moment the difference in their ages seemed supremely unimportant. But maybe Rhodri felt differently. Her mouth drooped as she contemplated a future without seeing Rhodri again. Like this, anyway. The big warm kitchen was an unusual place for a dinner-date, but in many ways far more dangerous than the restaurant of the Afon Arms. There was an alarming degree of intimacy in being alone together in such unlooked-for domesticity. Hilary leaned her head back against a cushion, watching Rhodri

through her lashes as he dealt with the dishes at top
speed. To her surprise he even put them away in what
were obviously the right places.

'You're very efficient,' she commented, when Rhodri
let himself down beside her at last, stretching his long
legs out in front of him.

'I visit the Thomases regularly. Mary always insists I
eat a meal with them so I always insist I help wash up.'
He smiled at her surprised expression. 'I suppose you
imagined I always ate in restaurants?'

Hilary nodded. 'And certainly never washed any
dishes.'

'Who do you think does it when I'm in Oxford?'

She looked blank. 'I don't know. Don't you have any
staff?'

'Not live-in staff. I've got someone to come in and
clean and see to the laundry, but that's all.'

Hilary had somehow pictured a discreet army of ser-
vants somewhere in the background, and said so,
laughing a little as Rhodri reached out and chucked her
under the chin with a playful fist.

'I'm really an excessively ordinary chap,' he informed
her smugly.

Hilary roared with laughter. 'Apart from the pedigree, the life-style and that air of assurance of yours,
you mean!'

Rhodri's eyes narrowed. 'Are you making fun of me,
Miss Mason?'

'Do you mind?'

'No.'

'Good.'

They smiled at each other, then their eyes locked and
both smiles faded, and Hilary looked away quickly, sen-
sitive to the change of atmosphere.

'I should go home,' she said hastily, looking at her watch. 'Mr and Mrs Thomas will probably be home soon.'

'It's early. They won't be back for at least a couple of hours yet.'

'Oh.' Hilary kept her eyes on her hands.

'Are you afraid to be alone here with me like this?'

'Not afraid, exactly.'

'Then why are your hands trembling?' He slid across the space between them and turned her face up to his. 'I'll admit the situation is far more suited to seduction than our previous time together. No one knows we're here, or even that you and I are together.'

'We were probably seen leaving the hotel, don't worry,' she assured him, annoyed because she sounded so breathless.

'But no one knows we *stayed* together. I'm assumed to be on my way to Oxford——' Rhodri paused, his eyes glittering down into hers. 'Unless you were expected somewhere this evening?'

Hilary shook her head slowly. 'No.'

'Then it seems a great shame to waste such a golden— and unique—opportunity, don't you think?'

'Aren't you overlooking something, Rhodri?'

'What do you mean?' His eyes narrowed to crystalline slivers between the thick fringe of lashes.

'The small matter of my age, Mr Lloyd-Ellis. It's only a few weeks more than it was last time we met.' Hilary returned his look unwaveringly, and he put out a hand to touch her untidy hair.

'Shall I tell you something?' he said conversationally. 'I've come to realise, since that night you mention, that time will inevitably solve the problem of your age, and that in the meantime I refuse to let it serve as an obstacle to the enjoyment of occasions like these. Do you agree?'

'I'm not sure. Just what did you have in mind?' she whispered.

'I thought we'd just stay here together, like this,' and he slid his arm around her waist and drew her close, stroking her hair so that her head drooped automatically against his shoulder. 'We can talk a little, get to know each other better, and just enjoy each other's company in a privacy that's a bit hard to achieve in Penafon.'

Hilary found the musical voice and gentle, stroking hand very hypnotic. She relaxed in Rhodri's hold, sighing a little as he settled her more comfortably in the crook of his arm. She curled up in a ball, her feet tucked beneath her as she leaned against him for support, her hand lying trustingly on his chest. She could feel the steady thud of his heart against her palm, and liked it. She liked the entire situation a lot, and smiled to herself as she remembered how angry she'd been with Rhodri earlier.

'What's so amusing?' he asked softly.

'I was thinking how strange it was to be here with you like this, when this morning I could have murdered you, preferably with my bare hands.'

He chuckled. 'Didn't I know it! Have you forgiven me?'

'How could I do otherwise when you've fed me, tucked me up for a nap, plied me with bacon and eggs and crowned it all by washing up?' Hilary raised her face to laugh into his eyes. 'You certainly know how to soften a girl up, Rhodri Lloyd-Ellis!'

'My intention was to feed you and make you listen to reason,' he retorted, and waved his free hand at his surroundings. 'All this was by way of a bonus. When you were sleeping this afternoon I had a brainwave when I thought of asking if Mary could feed us, and at the time, believe it or not, *this* part of it never occurred to me.'

Hilary searched his face, then nodded. 'I do believe you.' She snuggled her cheek back against his shoulder and wriggled a little to get more comfortable. 'This is lovely. Warmth and good food——'

'And an armistice,' said Rhodri, laughing, and squeezed her. 'I really thought you were about to do me an injury when I made off with you in the car.'

'Hardly practical when you were zooming off down the road like Alain Prost. My main thought was to fasten myself in, in case you landed us in the ditch!'

'But you were blazingly angry. It was radiating from you—I felt scorched. Are you still angry with me?'

'No. I wish you hadn't given me the push at the hotel, but I've cooled down enough to see why you did it.' Hilary pushed herself away to grin up at him mischievously. 'The pay wasn't very good, anyway!'

Rhodri gave a shout of laughter and shook her hard. 'Utter cheek! After the bonus I put in with your pay-packet, too.'

'Bonus?' Hilary frowned. 'What do you mean?'

'Didn't you open the envelope?'

She shook her head. 'It's in my bag in the car.'

Rhodri shrugged. 'I added a little extra when Erica was making up your money.'

Hilary's eyes narrowed. 'I'm not sure I like that. Sounds like hush money.'

He raised his eyes ceilingwards in exasperation. 'It was by way of a helping hand. If you don't want the cash, give it to charity.'

'Oh, I'm not proud,' she assured him. 'I'm afraid in this case charity really does begin at home. My home. So thank you kindly Mr Lloyd-Ellis. Your humble employee is deeply grateful.' And Hilary slid from his grasp and sank into a deep obeisance in front of him, the effect slightly marred by her lack of skirt to carry it off with the panache it deserved.

Rhodri reached out and seized her, dragging her back beside him, his face suddenly angry. 'Cut it out, Hilary. I'm a bit tired of this chip you've got on your shoulder. The main difference between us is not social, but financial. And anyone can earn money given sufficient education and opportunity.'

'*Your* education and opportunity, perhaps.'

He shook her again, not nearly so gently this time. 'Stop that! Instead, turn your attention to another difference between us, Hilary. A very big difference.'

She stared up at him with resigned blue eyes. 'You're not going to get boring about my age again, I hope.'

Rhodri smiled, a slow, disturbing smile Hilary viewed with alarm. 'No. Quite simply, my dear child, you are female and I am male. And as far as I'm concerned that's the only difference between us which is the slightest bit relevant at this moment in time.' And he pulled her against him and kissed her hard to underline his statement.

Hilary pulled away, breathless, her eyes brilliant with resentment as they glared up into his. 'I can do without the Tarzan and Jane bit, thank you!'

'Don't be childish,' he said negligently, and secured her against him with an arm muscular from years of regular squash games and sessions in a gym. He held her chin in his free hand, smiling down into her captive face. 'I just happen to be a man, and you, my dear Miss Mason, if not exactly a woman yet, are certainly a girl whom I find extraordinarily tempting, despite the freckles and the generous curves and the lack of inches and the deplorable temper. In which case, wouldn't you feel rather insulted if I *didn't* want to kiss you?'

Hilary tried to wriggle free, but he held her fast.

'Well?' he demanded, beginning to breathe a little faster. 'Am I not right? And while we're on the subject, can you honestly—honestly, I repeat—say you dislike the thought of being kissed by me?'

She opened her mouth to deny it fervently, then met the look in his eyes, saw the dark-rimmed irises bright with sudden heat, and she wavered. Honestly, he'd said. Which meant telling the truth. And the truth was that suddenly it was the most desirable thing in the world to be held like this and give herself up to all the kisses he wanted.

'No,' she said huskily.

Rhodri's lids dropped to veil his eyes. 'Does that mean no, you don't want me to kiss you?'

'No,' she repeated, her voice dropping to a whisper. 'I mean no, I can't deny I want you to kiss me, so——'

She got no further, the rest of her words smothered as their lips met and clung and opened to each other, breath and tongues mingled as their arms tightened about each other and they kissed with a mounting passion which took them both in its grip and rendered them helpless. With an inarticulate murmur Rhodri gently pulled her flat and lay beside her, turning her in his arms so that they lay mouth to mouth and breast to breast, each straining the other closer as blood drummed in unison in their ears.

They broke apart to stare at each other, grey eyes boring into blue as they breathed like marathon runners, then Rhodri's mouth met hers again and Hilary gave a little purr of sheer pleasure as his hands slid beneath her sweater and moved delicately over the smooth warm skin beneath it. Utterly ravished by the touch of his hard, warm mouth she moved her head from side to side as his lips slid down her throat while he pushed the collar of her sweater aside to search out the pulse which throbbed for him there. She gave a shudder of electrified surprise as hot reaction to his touch burned in places she had never considered connected in any way with her throat. She moaned and wriggled closer, pushing her hips against him, then jumped away in panic as she felt his unmistakable hard response thrust against her through their clothes.

'Don't be frightened,' he said hoarsely against her mouth. 'I promise to stop at kisses. Somehow. But, as I said before, I'm only a poor mortal male, and since you're all woman it's impossible to control *all* my responses.'

Hilary flushed hectically, but let him draw her close again, burrowing her face into his neck at the sudden impulse to throw caution to the winds and beg him to do anything he liked with her. No longer frightened by the intrusive proof of how much he wanted her, she ground her hips against him, fiercely glad when he groaned and thrust a hand into her hair, pulling her head back so he could kiss her deeply again and again, demanding and receiving a response which quickly threatened to get out of control.

'Oh, hell,' he said raggedly at last, pushing her away to stare into her heavy eyes. 'This must stop. Now. Or I won't answer for the consequences.'

Hilary nodded speechlessly, her breath coming in great gasps. 'I had no idea——' she gasped, wide-eyed. 'How about you?'

Rhodri swung his legs to the floor and pulled her into the crook of his arm, smiling down ruefully into her flushed face. 'Shall we say I know very well how quickly kisses can lead to more dangerous pastimes. What I didn't know was just how violently I'd react to your——'

'Enthusiasm?' she suggested, making a face.

He shook his head, stroking her tangled hair gently, as their breathing slowed. 'I wonder if you can understand how a man feels when his lovemaking evokes such a storm of response in a woman? It makes him feel like a lion, king of the jungle, and it's bloody hard trying to make a U-turn on the sort of road you and I were just travelling on, Hilary. Being a man of my word, I managed—just—to put on the brakes. But don't for a minute think it was easy.'

'I know it wasn't,' said Hilary, leaning against him trustingly. 'Because if it had been left to me I'm ashamed to say I wouldn't have been able to put on any brakes.'

'I suppose you realise you're paying me a very great compliment?'

'It's the unvarnished truth, Rhodri.'

'Which is why it's so flattering.'

Hilary looked up at him, biting her lip. 'I don't normally react to men like that.'

'I know.' He bent to kiss her on the tip of her nose. 'I saw you in action against Probert, remember.'

'Why is it so different?' she said, frowning. 'When he kissed me I was furious. With you I just want you to go on kissing me.'

'Which is a statement so bad for my blood pressure I'm going to take you home right now before I start kissing you again.' Rhodri sprang up, pulling her with him, and gave the lie to his words by taking her in his arms and kissing her several times before they finally left the warmth of Mary Thomas's kitchen.

'What's the name of the farm?' asked Hilary, once they were on the way back to Penafon.

Rhodri seemed to hesitate. 'Cwmderwen Farm,' he said after a while.

Hilary glanced at him quickly. 'It used to be yours then?'

He gave a deep sigh. 'I hate to admit it, but I'm afraid the Thomases are only tenant farmers. My tenants, to be precise.'

Hilary's smile was wry. 'Yet you wash the dishes in Mrs Thomas's kitchen.'

'I used to when I was a lad, and I see no reason to change now. Mary's the salt of the earth.'

'I'm sure she is. But I see now why she gave you the run of her kitchen—*droit de seigneur* and all that.'

'I think that covered a different type of subject altogether,' he said, laughing. 'And don't mention your fancy French phrases in front of Bryn Thomas, because he's very well read and would probably raise hell, even if Mary is a grandmother. We Celts are jealous of our women, you know.'

Hilary was surprised to hear the clock in the church tower strike ten as Rhodri stopped the car in Glebe Row. 'It's quite early, really,' she said, as she unfastened her seatbelt.

'Very true. No one can point a finger at you for staying out late.' Rhodri smiled at her and raised a hand to her lips. 'I'm not coming up those stairs tonight, Hilary. My self-control has been tested over and above the call to-night already, and if I come up there with you I might not be so noble a second time.'

'Couldn't you kiss me goodnight here?' she asked simply.

'Oh, yes,' he breathed, pulling her into his arms. 'With the utmost pleasure.' The kiss went on for so long that they were both shaken when they tore themselves apart.

'I'd better go.' Hilary turned blindly to open the door of the car while Rhodri reached into the back for her tote bag. He got out and came round to give it to her, holding something else in the other hand.

'You'd better have a look at this,' he said in an odd voice.

Hilary peered at it in the darkness. 'What is it?'

'The rotor arm of your Mini.'

She snatched it from him and glared up at his wary face. 'You mean you deliberately put my car out of action?'

'To put it another way,' he said swiftly, 'I was determined to get you to spend some time with me, one way or another, so making sure your car wouldn't start seemed like the best way to achieve it.'

'And just how,' she asked with hostility, 'am I supposed to get the rotor arm back in the Mini? I'm no mechanic.'

'Don't worry. I'll sneak back to the hotel now and see to it myself while no one's about, only then, of course, there's the problem of getting the car back to you.'

Hilary gave an exasperated little snort. 'I'll just have to go up there on the bus tomorrow and collect it.'

Rhodri leaned against the stair railing. 'I won't say I'm sorry, because frankly, sweetheart, I'm not. I've never enjoyed a day more, even if my companion did go off to sleep in the middle of it.'

Hilary relented, laughing up at him. 'Sorry about that.'

'The evening which followed was a quite miraculous recompense,' he said softly, and she felt her cheeks grow hot.

'I'd better go in,' she said breathlessly, and took her bag from him, smiling a little shyly. 'Thank you for the day, Rhodri. I enjoyed it enormously too.'

'All of it?'

'Yes. All of it. Goodnight.' Conscious that his eyes followed her, Hilary ran swiftly up her spiral staircase, leaning over the landing rail to wave goodbye before she unlocked her door and switched on the lights.

She felt absurdly happy as she filled the kettle and rummaged in a tin for a biscuit to eat with her coffee while she watched an old black and white film on her new television. During one of the commercial breaks she suddenly remembered her pay-packet and took the envelope out of her bag. There was the usual slip with a record of her earnings, which were exactly as she'd expected for the time put in. But there was also a smaller sealed envelope, with her name written in a hand she remembered from the only time she'd seen it before, on an invitation she'd never received.

Hilary tore it open, her eyes goggling as she found several banknotes in a folded sheet of paper with a note signed with the initial R.

'I'm worried about you. Please accept this to tide you over while I find some less exhausting way for you to earn pocket-money.'

CHAPTER EIGHT

WHEN she got back to work at the library Hilary was obliged to put up with a lot of eager questions from Olwen about the reception at the hotel. She responded sketchily, adding, 'You were wrong, by the way. Rhodri Lloyd-Ellis still owns Cwmderwen Court, only someone else runs it for him.'

Olwen looked at her in surprise. 'I didn't know that!' She hesitated. 'Actually he owns quite a lot of property round here, you know, Hilary. Very well thought of, Rhodri, in these parts. It beats me why an attractive man like him is still single.'

Hilary reached up to the top shelf of As as she began shelving a pile of books. 'He was engaged once, wasn't he?' she asked casually.

'You mean that business with Sarah Morgan, the Rector of Cwmderwen's daughter?' Olwen shrugged. 'Flash in the pan, that was. One minute they were at her sister's wedding, like a couple of turtledoves. Next minute Sarah was getting married—in the same church, mind you—to the man she worked for. Very fishy, or so people thought in Cwmderwen.'

Hilary would have liked to hear more, but an influx of borrowers put an end to their chat. By the time there was a lull Olwen was full of the new baby one of her neighbours had produced over Easter, after which it was hard to bring up the subject of Rhodri's former *amours* again without attracting comment. When the library closed she caught the bus that passed Cwmderwen Court Hotel and walked up the long drive, feeling uncomfortably furtive as she opened the Mini and slid behind the wheel, glad that it was the run-up to the dinner-hour, and no one she knew was in sight. She made her getaway quickly, eager to get home in case Rhodri rang.

The telephone rang several times later that evening, and Hilary sprang up to answer it eagerly each time, trying hard not to sound too disappointed when the first time it was Candida, asking about her weekend, then later it was her parents on the same subject, until finally, gratifyingly, the voice she was hoping for said 'Hello' in her ear.

'How are you today, Hilary?' Rhodri asked.

'Just fine. And you?'

'Ditto. Did you collect the Mini?'

'Yes. I felt as if I were stealing the wretched thing! But I managed to make off with it without being seen.'

'I'm glad. I wouldn't care to risk that temper of yours too often.'

'It's not that bad!'

'Not bad! You're talking to a chap who has not only been on the receiving end of your hockey-stick, but happened to be an eye-witness of your impressive right hook, young lady!'

Hilary giggled. 'I'm quite harmless really.'

'I wouldn't say that,' he said, in a tone that made her knees tremble. 'Making love to you has very harmful side-effects. I've been suffering withdrawal symptoms all day. Very distressing in the middle of a board meeting. I kept thinking of the way you felt in my arms, of your mouth opening under mine——'

'Stop, stop!' she begged, her heart pounding, and Rhodri laughed.

'That's not what you said last night!'

'That's not fair! Besides,' she added, 'I don't know that I'm very pleased with *you*.'

'With me, or my kisses?'

'Will you be serious?'

'Believe me—I am.'

'I'm talking about the money you gave me. It doesn't seem right.'

It was Rhodri's turn to pause. 'Since I gave it to you beforehand,' he said slowly, 'surely you can't believe it had anything to do with what happened afterwards?'

'Good lord, no—I didn't mean that.' Hilary flushed scarlet at the thought. 'Besides, I thought money only changed hands when there was rather more than mere kissing involved.'

'I really wouldn't know,' he assured her innocently. 'But if the money troubles you, just look on it as a loan, and pay it back when your fortunes improve.'

'I really feel I should give it back now,' said Hilary severely.

'Don't do that. Please.'

'All right—then thank you, Rhodri. I'll add it to my savings.'

'What are you saving for, exactly?'

'A rainy day, I suppose. Goodnight. Thank you for ringing.'

'Goodnight, Hilary. Make sure you lock your door before you go to sleep.'

Hilary went to bed feeling very pleased with life, until it occurred to her that Rhodri had said nothing about any future meeting. Even then she felt philosophical, reasonably sure that he meant them to meet again. Otherwise why would he bother to ring and say such ego-boosting things to her?

She was right. A couple of evenings later he rang again.

'Do you think you could cadge a bed from your sister this weekend?' he asked. 'I think I have the answer to your cash-flow problem, provided you come down here and talk to a chap I know.'

'If the job's in Oxford it's not much use,' she said doubtfully.

Rhodri gave an exasperated sigh. 'Credit me with enough sense to realise that, my darling child. This is something you can do in your spare time at home, but I won't elaborate until you've met the chap in question. He just happens to be in Oxford this weekend, visiting one of his offspring.'

'Curiouser and curiouser,' said Hilary, laughing, and promised to let him know as soon as she could.

Candida was only too pleased at the prospect of a visit from her sister, particularly when she heard Rhodri was at the bottom of it.

'Of course you can come,' she said, intrigued when she heard the reason. 'But what on earth is this work Rhodri's getting you to do at home? Sounds faintly disreputable.'

'I'm not opening a massage-parlour!' Hilary assured her with a giggle. 'You can bet your boots it'll be highly respectable if Rhodri's behind it.'

'Because he's such a "parfit gentil knight", you mean?'

Hilary thought for a moment. 'Yes. I think you've hit the nail on the head, sister dear. He's a man of rather high principles, unless I'm utterly mistaken. Of course I could be wrong, but I don't think so.'

'Unlike his second cousin once removed, or whatever Jack is,' said Candida bitterly. 'He's quite the reverse. I can't open a magazine these days without seeing pictures of Jack draped round the female lead in his wretched play.'

'I expect he has to do that,' said Hilary practically. 'Good for publicity.'

'But very bad for my own peace of mind. Anyway, never mind all that, what time will you be here on Saturday?'

It was well into the afternoon the following weekend by the time Hilary managed to get away, and since the Mini rattled rather ominously at anything over fifty miles an hour it was late enough for Candida to be worried by the time her sister parked the car at her gate. She flew out of the house instantly, scolding as Hilary got out and gave her a hug.

'Where have you been? I've been walking up and down in there for ages imagining all sorts of things.'

'Hello, love. Sorry I'm a bit late, but I had a slow journey. This old banger doesn't like it if I try to hurry. You know that.'

'Rhodri rang,' said Candida, as they went inside. 'He'll be round later.'

While they drank tea, Candida was full of questions about the job and life in Penafon, delicately leaving out all references to Rhodri until Hilary brought up the subject herself. Candida's magnificent eyes started out of her head when she learnt that not only was he the owner of the best hotel in the area round Penafon, but that her sister had been working there in her spare time and had been summarily sacked the moment Rhodri laid eyes on her, once he realised she was in one of the hotel uniforms and had a tray of drinks in her hand. Candida gave her sister a trenchant lecture on being silly enough to take on two jobs at once, and looked very impressed when she heard Rhodri had taken such exception to the idea.

'He must—well, like you, Hilly.'

'I think he does.'

Candida eyes her narrowly. 'And you like *him*?'

'Of course,' said Hilary airily. 'Who wouldn't? But since I've never had a crush on any man before, I'm sure it isn't something I won't get over after—afterwards.'

'Let's hope so,' said Candida, sounding bitter again. 'It doesn't do to fall in love, believe me. It's a highly overrated pastime.'

Since she seemed disinclined to say more on the subject Hilary made no mention of Jack Wynne Jones, afraid to ask if he'd been in contact of late in case he hadn't. She changed the subject to ask about Nell, who was a staff nurse at the John Radcliffe Hospital.

'It's her nights off this weekend so she's driven home to her parents in Coventry. We've got the place to ourselves,' said Candida. 'I don't see much of her anyway. She's getting very pally with the new Orthopod boy-wonder at the hospital these days—spends most of the spare time she gets with him when she can.' She jumped up as the telephone rang, her eyes suddenly bright as she glanced at the clock. The light in them dimmed a little as she answered the phone, then held it out to Hilary. 'It's for you, love—I'll pop upstairs to change.'

'Hello,' said Hilary cautiously, as she watched her sister's rather dejected progress up the stairs.

'At last!' said Rhodri. 'You took your time getting there, Hilary.'

'*Et tu, Brute?* I've just had Candida on the same subject. My Mini's a bit less speedy than your chariot, remember?'

'Well, now you've finally made it get your skates on, because I've got this chap coming round. The only snag is that I don't know quite when and I'm impatient to see you again. Instead of making me wait, could you possibly persuade your Mini to crawl the extra mile over here, Hilary?'

The thought of Rhodri's impatience gave Hilary such a boost that she would have crawled the mile on her hands and knees. 'I think I could,' she said, perfectly casual, then bit her lip. 'But, Rhodri, could I ask you a favour?'

'Anything in the world!' he said promptly.

Hilary's toes curled in her tennis shoes at his tone, and she gave a breathless little chuckle. 'Rash man! All I'm asking is whether you'd mind if Candida came too, this evening. She seems a bit down.'

'Didn't she tell you I'd already asked her?'

'No, she didn't.' Hilary smiled brightly, forgetting he couldn't see her. 'Great, that's settled then, just tell me where we find you.'

After she'd put the phone down Hilary went upstairs to the small spare-room, feeling oddly flat. Of course Rhodri had invited Candida too. Why shouldn't he? She unpacked the few belongings she'd brought, and hung them up in the tiny closet, then jumped as Candida tapped her on the shoulder.

'Did Rhodri tell you he'd asked me along this evening as well?' asked her sister.

Hilary nodded, and smiled. 'Yes. Great.'

'Don't sound so enthusiastic! Apparently my presence is required because it's a sort of glorified blind date.'

'*What?*'

'That's right. This man he's invited round is divorced and at a loose end in Oxford. Rhodri obviously thinks I would round out the quartet.' Candida shrugged. 'Why not? It's better than sitting at home alone with my knitting.' She grabbed Hilary by the hand. 'Talking of knitting, I've made you something.'

Hilary laughed, letting herself be pulled along the landing to Candida's bedroom to give her opinion on a knitted tunic and skirt laid out on the bed.

'There!' said Candida in triumph. 'What do you think?'

Hilary picked up the long tunic and laid it against herself in the mirror. She smoothed a hand over it lovingly, and gave her sister an excited smile. 'It's perfect! You're so clever.'

'I was sure that shade would match your hair. Try it on. I think I got the size right.'

Hilary dashed off to shower first, then put on the beige satin teddy Candida insisted on lending her, and a pair of ultra-thin stockings she'd been hoarding for a special occasion, finally pulling on the rather short, narrow skirt, which her sister had knitted in fine vertical rib for a perfect fit. Candida lowered the tunic over her sister's curly head, looking very smug as Hilary smoothed it over her hips. It was long and plain and very flattering, even to Hilary's self-critical eyes.

'It's wonderful,' she said, and hugged her sister. 'Thank you.'

'Just don't tell anyone *I* made it, there's a good girl, and I'll let you borrow my blue beads to wear with it!'

In all the excitement of the new outfit they were a little late by the time they arrived in the quiet, tree-lined road where Rhodri lived.

'Is this the place?' asked Candida, peering through the tall iron gates at the solid-looking house beyond its small square of lawn.

'Yes. Big, isn't it?' said Hilary gloomily as she locked the car.

'Very nice indeed,' said Candida, impressed. 'Come on, muggins, stop hanging back.' She pushed her sister through the gates in front of her, then pressed the bell she found beside one of the double glass doors. Rhodri opened it instantly, as though he'd been standing waiting on the other side for them to arrive.

He kissed both girls before drawing them into the hall Hilary remembered so well from her first, less auspicious visit.

'Hello,' she said, pink and breathless from Rhodri's kiss, which had been considerably more lingering than the one he gave Candida.

'You're late!' he said accusingly, then whistled in admiration as he took their coats. 'Not that the wait wasn't worth it. Both of you are a sheer delight to the eyes.'

Candida was wearing one of her own creations, a dress knitted in fine black wool, with no ornament whatsoever, other than her own hair and skin, and looked as she always looked, utterly beautiful.

'Thank you, Rhodri,' she said serenely. 'Right. Where's this man I'm supposed to entertain?'

He laughed, and slid his arm through Hilary's. 'Actually he isn't here. He made the mistake of taking a nap after a long, liquid lunch with his son, and just rang to say he's only just surfaced, so I said we'd meet him later in the foyer of the Randolph, then go off in search of a drink and supper.'

Ignoring Hilary's disapproving frown, Candida asked if they could look round the ground floor of the house, and kept Hilary firmly at her side as Rhodri took them on a quick tour of high-ceilinged rooms with tall windows, furnished, he told them, with various pieces taken from Cwmderwen Court before it became a hotel.

Candida was loud with approval as they returned to the drawing-room for drinks, but Hilary said nothing at all, feeling rather depressed. The house matched its owner. It had the same air of casual, taken-for-granted elegance.

'Do you like my home, Hilary?' asked Rhodri in an undertone, while Candida admired the collection of porcelain in a boulle cabinet on the far side of the room.

'Very much. It suits you.'

He eyed her quizzically. 'I wonder what you mean by that.'

Hilary had no intention of explaining that it daunted her a little, and was glad when Candida rejoined them, demanding to know something about the man they were to meet later.

'His name's Drew Redman,' said Rhodri. 'One of the pies he has his fingers in is printing. Which is where Hilary comes in.'

'How?' she asked, mystified.

'I'll let him explain that himself.'

To Hilary's surprise a taxi came to collect them a little later.

'So I can have a drink without worrying about the drive home,' explained Rhodri. 'Don't worry, Hilary. Your car will be perfectly safe where it is.'

'Even safer if I whip out the rotor arm,' she said drily.

Candida looked puzzled. 'That's sounds very technical!'

'You'd be surprised,' said her sister cryptically, and threw a shining blue glance up at Rhodri.

'We'll enlarge later,' he said, laughing, and helped both girls on with their coats.

Hilary never tired of witnessing Candida's impact on a man meeting her her for the first time. Drew Redman wore an expression of utter disbelief when he greeted them in the foyer of the Randolph Hotel. He was very dark, greying a little at the temples, and slimly built, with a fine-boned face and dark eyes which Hilary decided were probably very intelligent when not wearing their present dazed look.

'How—how do you do?' he said, forgetting to let go of Candida's hand.

Candida gave him a smile which routed him even further. 'Did you have a nice sleep, Mr Redman? I gather lunch with your son put you out for the count.'

His answering smile was rueful. 'One of the penalties of encroaching middle age, I'm afraid. A nap now and then becomes not only desirable, but necessary!'

Rhodri laughed and clapped him on the back. 'Come on, Methuselah. Can you manage to stagger through the town? I thought we'd take a walk before having a drink and some supper at the Turf Tavern.'

Drew Redman looked rather taken aback. 'Wouldn't you prefer dinner here?' He was looking at Candida as he spoke, obviously convinced the Randolph was more suited to someone of her type than the pub Rhodri had in mind.

'Not in the least,' she said, a shadow dimming her smile fleetingly. 'I'm sure Hilary would love somewhere less formal. So would I.'

'Then the Turf it is,' he said gallantly.

Hilary enjoyed their stroll through the spring evening, as they made their leisurely way along Broad Street in the fading light, happy to renew her acquaintance with the mysterious carved heads encircling the Sheldonian Theatre as they passed by. Drew Redman walked ahead with Candida, who was obviously charming him out of his wits with her company, without the least effort on her part.

'Drew seems to have forgotten about encroaching decrepitude,' murmured Rhodri with a grin, as he fell back with Hilary, who was looking about her in frank tourist fashion as they wandered along.

She smiled. 'He's really quite young, isn't he? How old is this son of his?'

'Your age, miss. Which, just in case you hadn't thought of it, makes Drew old enough to be *your* father too,' he reminded her.

Hilary gave him a rather cheeky little smile. 'Does it really? Do you look on me in a paternal way too?'

Rhodri scowled and began walking more quickly, so that Hilary had to break into a trot to keep up. 'No,' he said shortly. 'I do not.'

They caught up with the others in Bath Place, where Hilary forgot the momentary loss of harmony, seizing Rhodri's hand as she exclaimed about the cobbles and the charming pastel houses leaning at odd angles to each other. Then they took a left turn through a narrow, low archway into the garden of the Turf Tavern, which was tucked away under the towering city wall, in the shadow of the bell tower of New College.

'Though it seems strange to call it "New", when it's been here for six centuries,' remarked Candida as her smile cleared a way for them through the crowded, cosy pub, and ensured somewhere for the four of them to sit down.

'The term new is relative in Oxford. I believe it dates back to the thirteenth century, like this place,' said Rhodri, putting an arm round Hilary to steady himself.

She loved the inn, looking round her eagerly at the head-splitting beams and drinking in the atmosphere with an open enjoyment both men viewed with exchanged smiles. She nodded to all the suggestions Rhodri made regarding food, and afterwards had no idea what she'd eaten, too taken up with the novelty of her surroundings and the hot mulled cider she was given to drink to notice the meal very much.

'As you can see,' said Candida drily to Drew Redman, 'my sister's taste quite definitely runs to this sort of thing rather than the more formal delights of the Randolph.'

He laughed and leaned across to talk directly to Hilary. 'I gather you're a librarian somewhere in the wilds of Wales, according to Rhodri.'

She nodded. 'Lovely little place called Penafon—but a lot quieter than this!'

'With lots of time to yourself in the evenings?'

'Absolutely. Though I do have a television now,' she added, eyes sparkling. 'It makes an enormous difference to my long, lonely evenings!'

'You didn't have one when you moved in?' asked Rhodri, frowning.

'No. But never mind that. Rhodri tells me you might have some kind of work I could do at home, Mr Redman.'

'Oh, Drew, please—unless you want me to feel a hundred years old,' he protested.

'You look the same age as me,' said Rhodri blandly. 'I have it on the best authority.'

Candida gave a smothered laugh, and shook her head at Hilary.

'I know exactly how old you are, Rhodri,' said Hilary crisply, and turned back to Drew, who explained that some of his business interests were concerned with high-class wedding-stationery.

Hilary was intrigued to find all she'd be required to do was to buy daily broadsheets like *The Times* and *Telegraph* every day, then go through the forthcoming weddings and confirm the addresses of the bride-to-be's parents on a supply of microfiche, the sheets of film which, in this case, had addresses recorded on them.

'I'll provide you with the necessary screen you need to scan them,' said Drew, 'then you see which people are the most likely prospects for our wedding-pack.' He smiled. 'It's not much use if the bride lives in Timbuktu, of course.'

'So all you want is for me to sift through the papers each evening and send you a list of likely addresses?' asked Hilary.

'Yes. Every few days or so would do. I'll pay you a reasonable amount per hour, and perhaps you could put in eight to ten hours a week.' Drew grinned as Hilary's face lit up. 'It'll probably bore you after a while, I'm afraid.'

'No more than waiting on table and running up and down stairs with trays of early-morning tea,' said Rhodri trenchantly.

'Very true,' agreed Candida. 'It sounds tailor-made for Hilary, Drew. Thank you.'

For a moment Hilary felt a twinge of resentment as the other three busily sorted out her life for her, but she suppressed it quickly, thanking Drew so prettily that he reached across and patted her hand.

'Hi, Dad!' said a voice behind them, and Drew jumped to his feet, flushing slightly as a tall young man edged his way round the table and stood at his elbow, smiling expectantly as he waited to be introduced.

'Didn't think I'd run into you tonight, Andrew,' said his father, looking slightly flustered. 'I thought you were tied up with friends. These beautiful ladies are Miss Candida Mason and her sister Hilary, and of course you already know Rhodri Lloyd-Ellis.'

The young man acknowledged the introductions gracefully, and managed to produce a stool from somewhere which he wedged next to Hilary. To the latter's surprise young Andrew Redman seemed more taken with herself than Candida, whom he left to talk to the other men while he questioned Hilary eagerly on her presence in Oxford and anything else she might care to tell him about herself. He was very dark, like his father, with bright hazel eyes that examined Hilary feature by feature with unabashed interest. He was reading English at Brasenose, he informed her, and within the space of minutes Hilary found herself plunged into a discussion on modern American literature which she enjoyed so much that she was rather startled when Rhodri tapped her on the shoulder.

'I repeat, Hilary,' he said curtly, 'what would you like to drink?'

'Oh, orange juice, or something,' she said vaguely, and turned back to Andrew Redman. 'But you know, I disagree with you there—from Toni Morrison's *Beloved* I received a whole new concept of slavery...'

And they were off again, deep in the throes of an argument which lasted until Candida reached over to interrupt. 'Time, children. We're leaving now, Hilary.'

Hilary jumped up, embarrassed, as she saw the wooden look on Rhodri's face and realised she'd spent the best part of an hour deep in conversation with Andrew, without a word to any of the others.

'Sorry! I get carried away sometimes, I'm afraid.'

'It's been great,' said Andrew, apparently unaware of any coolness in the atmosphere. 'How long are you staying in Oxford?'

'Only until tomorrow,' Hilary told him, very conscious now of glacial vibrations coming at her from Rhodri's direction. 'I enjoyed our talk. Goodbye.'

The young man looked eager to say more, but Drew Redman gave his son a quelling look.

'You'd better get back to your friends, Andrew,' he said quietly. 'I'll expect you for breakfast at the hotel at nine-thirty tomorrow. I'd like to get off by mid-morning.'

Hilary felt subdued on the walk back to the Randolph, where they waited in the cocktail bar for the taxi Rhodri ordered. It was so obvious that neither Rhodri nor

Candida were at all pleased that Hilary made very little contribution to the conversation, only pretending to sip at a ginger ale she didn't want until it was time to go. In the taxi on the way back Rhodri made no attempt to sit between herself and her sister, and when they reached Candida's house he told the taxi to wait for him, refusing Candida's invitation to coffee.

'I think I can hear my phone ringing,' said Candida tactfully. 'Goodnight, Rhodri, and thank you for a lovely evening.' She hurried into the house, leaving her sister to it.

Rhodri looked down at Hilary in the light of the porch, his face quite dauntingly austere. 'I'll bring the Mini over in the morning,' he said.

'Thank you.'

'What time do you intend setting off for Penafon?'

'I hadn't thought. Some time in the afternoon, I suppose.' Hilary stole an unhappy look at him. 'I really didn't mean to be rude tonight, Rhodri.'

He was silent for a moment. 'You weren't rude, exactly.' He thrust a hand through his hair. 'Perhaps it was a damn good thing, really. Seeing you with someone of your own age, I mean. Rather a timely reminder that fifteen years between us is a hell of an age-gap. One I'm not sure it's realistic to think we can bridge.'

Her blood ran cold. 'Do you really believe that?' she asked very quietly.

'It's a point to consider.' He touched her cheek fleetingly. 'The meter's running. I'd better go. See you in the morning.'

'Yes,' she said dully. 'Goodnight.' She watched his tall, graceful figure stride down the path to the gate, then turned and went in the house without waiting to see if he waved before he got in the taxi. From the withdrawn look on his handsome face it seemed unlikely he would, and Hilary quickly shut the door behind her, sure that even so small a rebuff would act like the final straw on the proverbial camel's back.

CHAPTER NINE

HILARY found she was angry rather than heartbroken as she tossed and turned restlessly in her sister's spare bed that night. It was maddening to remember that only a few short days earlier Rhodri had been so insistent that the only important difference between them was the male–female one, yet tonight, all of a sudden, just because she'd had a perfectly innocuous chat with Andrew Redman in the Turf Tavern, apparently all that was changed. Now, it seemed she was either too young for Rhodri, or he was too old for her. Something which hadn't troubled him in the slightest in the kitchen of Cwmderwen Farm, she thought, grinding her teeth.

She flung over on her back and stared stormily at the ceiling. It was glaringly obvious that her wisest course was to forget all about Rhodri Lloyd-Ellis. If she were honest he'd always been out of her league anyway, one way and another: older—far too much older, apparently—with his property all over the place, and his high-flying job, not to mention the earls nesting in his family tree. Not really the sort of man a little bookworm of a librarian would think of in her wildest dreams as—as a lover, if she had any sense at all.

She got up next day, determined to face the fact, to greet Rhodri in a light-hearted, casual kind of way when he brought back the car, so that he'd know she quite appreciated the fact that their friendship was just that. *If* that. Hilary felt she'd rather die than give him an inkling of the way she really felt. As if the end of the world was imminent.

Candida, however, diagnosed Hilary's early-morning gloom with accuracy.

'Probably because I feel the same,' she assured Hilary, over the coffee which was all either of them could face in the way of breakfast.

'Why in particular? Didn't you enjoy the evening? I thought Drew Redman was rather nice. And utterly bedazzled with you.'

'He *is* nice,' sighed Candida. 'But he's not Jack. And Jack, far from being bedazzled, as you put it, seems convinced I'm the original goodtime girl. What's more, I think the idiot still dreams of stealing Davy from Leo Seymour. Which would not be clever, because I'm pretty sure Leo would kill him if he even tried.'

'Whereas I've been told to go away and play with chums of my own age,' groaned Hilary. 'Which, no doubt, is a fair indication that Rhodri still hankers after the Rector's beautiful daughter, damn her. I probably pale horribly by comparison.'

'What a pair!' sighed Candida.

Hilary jumped up, suddenly restless. 'I think I'll walk down to the newsagents for another paper. I've read yours from cover to cover already.'

'Buy some chocolate, or something. Let's have a sinful bout of self-indulgence to comfort ourselves.'

'You're on!'

Hilary let off steam by covering the distance to the small row of shops nearby at a brisk run. In the newsagent's she bought a couple of Sunday papers and two large bars of chocolate, then took a longer route back at a more leisurely pace to enjoy the sun which had decided to break through the early-morning cloud. But as she walked along her mind kept straying to Rhodri, however much she tried to haul it in any other directions, and in her abstraction she found she'd taken a wrong turning.

To her annoyance it was almost half an hour before she found her way back to the road where Candida lived. Her heart gave a sudden thump as she saw the Mini parked outside, and she slowed down, taking deep, even breaths to steady herself. Idiot, she jeered. Play it cool. All you do is thank him prettily for his kindness, say how much you appreciate the introduction to Drew Redman, then get in the car and hightail it for Penafon as fast as you can go.

Hilary was so deep in her plan of action she nearly jumped out of her skin when a carrying voice with an exaggerated Cockney accent called, 'Hello, darlin'! Fancy a lift in my motor, then?'

She looked round in astonishment as a long, powder-blue car nosed to a stop beside her, parking with precision behind the Mini, and a tall figure sprang out of it, laughing at her.

'Jack!' she said in astonishment, her face lighting up at the sight of him. 'Where did you spring from?'

'My bed—very early,' he said smugly, as he opened the gate for her, looking in the sunshine like the answer to a maiden's prayer, in denims and white sweater, a broad grin on his face. 'Mind you, I bet I was chancing my arm just then, accosting you like that. You might have poked me one in the eye for my cheek!'

'I don't go round hitting every man I see, you know,' she said ruefully. 'Anyway, what on earth are you doing here? Candida didn't say you were coming.'

'I thought I'd give her a lovely surprise,' said Jack smugly, then raised a quizzical black eyebrow. 'Or won't she think it lovely?'

'Only one way to find out!' said Hilary, and used Candida's key to let herself into the house.

'Let's creep in and surprise her,' whispered Jack, and put a hand over Hilary's mouth as she opened it to protest. He pulled her with him as he flung open the sitting-room door, the laughter in his black eyes changing to wrath at the sight of Candida held close in Rhodri's embrace.

'Surprise, surprise!' Jack spat, in a voice his ecstatic fans would never have recognised.

Hilary's fists clenched as Candida and Rhodri sprang apart at the sight of them, the expression on Candida's face one of sheer horror, Rhodri's eyes merely amused until they met the accusation blazing in Hilary's. There was a hideous silence for a space of seconds, then Candida and Jack began to speak at once, she with a torrent of explanation, he with reiterated furious refusals to believe a word of it. Rhodri made no attempt to say anything, and Hilary flung out of the room and tore upstairs to pack her bag. She whirled round, eyes like blue flames as Rhodri strode into the small room after her, and slammed the door shut.

'It wasn't what you imagined,' he said without preamble.

'I may be *young*, but I'm not totally naïve!' she taunted. 'Not that it's any of my business, anyway.' She gave an angry little laugh. 'Mind you, I'd keep out of Jack's way for a bit. He looked fighting mad from where I was.'

Rhodri grabbed her by the elbows and shook her a little. 'Hilary, will you shut up and listen——'

'No! Why should I? It's no skin off my nose if you fancy cuddling Candida. Who could blame you? Only I'd better warn you you're on a losing wicket. She's really potty about Jack, you know.' She tried to break free, but Rhodri's long fingers bit into her skin, and she winced, her eyes flashing blue sparks at him. 'Bully!' she said bitterly. 'Give me my car-keys, please!'

'Not until you listen!' he grated.

'To what? I listened last night, remember. I'm too young, you said. We're not right for each other. Not that I ever thought we were,' she assured him, which was only the truth. 'And please don't think me ungrateful. Many thanks for putting me in touch with Drew Redman and the job, Rhodri, it was nice to meet him—not to mention his son! Anyway, I'm off back to Penafon now, so I don't suppose I'll see you again. Goodbye.'

Rhodri's eyes bored down into her defiant ones for a long, cold interval, then he raised a cynical eyebrow, and stepped back, shrugging.

'All right, Hilary. I get the message. As I've said before, possibly more than once, you still have a bloody great deal of growing up to do. Let me know when you've finally accomplished it.' He seized her again without warning and kissed her hard and long, then strode from the room, leaving her with a hand to her bruised mouth, and tears which welled up and spilled over to sting her scarlet cheeks as she stared in misery at the door Rhodri slammed shut behind him.

Hilary heard the front door bang, and ran to the window to see Rhodri sprint down the path, hurdle over the gate like Ed Moses, then leap into Jack's car. The engine started with a tigerish roar and Hilary winced, dashing away her tears as the car took off down the quiet road like a rocket. Rhodri must be blazing mad, she realised with satisfaction, to gun a beautiful car down the road like that. She sniffed hard and scrubbed at her eyes, managing a ghost of a chuckle at the thought that Jack would probably be blazing mad, too. His beloved car was a valuable E-Type Jaguar of some antiquity and value, and certain to be his pride and joy.

Hilary washed her face and did a little repair work to remove any traces of tears, then collected her jacket and weekend bag and decided it was safe to venture downstairs. She hung about for a while on the landing, listening to the voices from the sitting-room, both of them raised in impassioned argument even now, then sat down on the top stair, deciding she'd better wait until Candida and Jack had cooled before going down to say goodbye.

After a while the voices behind the closed door subsided. Hilary waited a minute or two longer then went down and opened the sitting-room door a crack to peer round it. Her eyes opened saucer-wide at the sight of Candida and Jack in such close embrace it was difficult to see where one ended and the other began. They were still fully clothed, but both of them wildly dishevelled as they strained together, kissing each other with such unrestrained ferocity that it was obvious to anyone with half an eye that the fully clothed bit was unlikely to prevail for long.

Removing herself smartly, Hilary tore a sheet from the telephone pad and wrote a hurried note to inform her sister that, in the circumstances, she was going back to Penafon sooner than planned. Then she let herself quietly out of the house and made her getaway.

It was a beautiful spring day, and at any other time Hilary would have enjoyed the drive back. As it was she spent the first half of the journey cooling down, and the second half castigating herself for the temper which had blinded her to the real reason for the scene she and Jack had interrupted, certain now it had been entirely innocent. Candida, for one, would never have allowed any familiarity from a man she knew her sister was in love with.

Hilary swallowed convulsively. In love with? She abandoned the thought hurriedly, and fell to wondering wistfully just exactly why Rhodri had been moved to take Candida in his arms. If he'd intended anything really heavy he was hardly fool enough to try it when little Hilary was about to put in an appearance at any minute. Just the same, Hilary desperately wished she'd let Rhodri explain, instead of flaring up at him like a silly kid. It was a long time before she could bring herself to smile, as she speculated on how things had progressed with Candida and Jack after she'd left.

Hilary wasn't left long in doubt. The telephone was ringing as she unlocked the door of her flat. She dumped her bag on the floor and went to answer it, not in the least surprised to hear Candida's voice on the line.

'Hilary! Where've you *been*?'

'Where do you think I've been! Driving back at my usual pace, of course.'

'You've been ages—I've been frantic. One way and another.' Candida's voice dropped. 'Look, darling, you didn't really think I was letting Rhodri make love to me, surely!'

'No. But I thought maybe he was *trying* to. What man wouldn't? But I never thought for a moment you were joining in, I promise.'

'I wish you'd stayed to convince Jack of that.'

'I peeped in at you on my way out. Jack looked excessively convinced to me.'

Candida let out a gurgle. 'Glory! I didn't realise you'd seen us.'

'It seemed wisest not to make my presence known.'

'Oh, Hilly, he says he wants to marry me.'

Hilary let out a war-whoop. 'Really? That's fantastic—when's the happy day?'

'Hold on. I didn't say yes.'

Hilary sat down cross-legged on the floor. 'Are you crazy? You've been fretting yourself to fiddlestrings about the man, and then you turn him down when he proposes?'

'It's not as simple as that,' said Candida soberly. 'I want to be sure he means it.'

'Does he make a habit of proposing to women?'

'No. He says that apart from Davy, I'm the only woman who's ever made him think of matrimony.'

'Ah, I see. It's the "apart from Davy" bit that's rocking your boat.' Hilary nodded her head unseen.

'Precisely. So as I thought we ought to simmer down a bit, Jack's gone jogging round to Rhodri's place to make sure Edna's all right——'

'*Who?*'

'Jack's car. Edna the E-Type.'

'Ah!' said Hilary darkly. 'Watch it, sister dear. *She's* your main rival, not Davy.'

'More than likely. And to be fair, Davy's no rival. Just a sort of innocent obstacle on my particular path of true love.'

Hilary laughed. 'Ugh, how florid!' She hesitated, then said diffidently, 'Tell me to mind my own business if you like, Candida, but did you two end up in bed this afternoon?'

There was silence on the other end of the line for a moment, then her sister said in a rather strained voice, 'Yes. When I found you'd taken off I started crying, and then Jack began to comfort me, and——'

'That was that. Surely it rather made up your mind for you?'

'It was bliss. But there's more to life than that, Hilary! I want Jack to like the other side of me.'

'How can he, when you keep it hidden like a skeleton in the closet?' Hilary had a sudden brainwave. 'Look, is Jack coming back there this evening?'

'Yes. He's taking me out for a meal.'

'Don't let him. Cook for him. Give him the beef you were intending to roast for me. Wear something you knitted with your own fair hands, and *tell* him you made it. Show him the real Candida Mason for once.'

'He'd probably run a mile,' wailed Candida.

'I doubt it. Go on. Be brave. Try it.'

It took several minutes to convince Candida it was a good idea, and several more to convince her that little Hilary wasn't in despair over Rhodri Lloyd-Ellis, before Candida went off to prepare a meal guaranteed to amaze her would-be bridegroom.

Hilary wished she had some sound advice for herself on a miracle cure for a dented heart. The only remedy she came up with was to keep herself occupied, and she was very pleased when a day or two later the promised supply of address-bearing microfiche arrived, along with the necessary viewer to read them. She threw herself into the new pastime with concentration, refusing Catrin's blandishments to share the takeaway suppers her young neighbour often brought home from Newport.

'Coffee later when I've finished,' promised Hilary, eyes glued to the screen. 'Work first, pleasure afterwards.'

For a while Hilary lived on a knife-edge of expectancy, waiting for Rhodri to ring. Every time she heard the trill of the telephone her heart did a somersault in her chest, and she needed a moment or two before she could speak normally to Candida, who was invariably on the other end of the line. Hilary was glad for her sister, who was nowadays floating on cloud nine, and deeply grateful to Hilary for making her reveal the real Candida Mason to

John Wynne Jones, star of stage and screen. To Hilary's amusement Candida had greeted her swain that first Sunday evening attired in a heavy-duty sweater fresh from her own needles, worn with a pair of rubbed old cords, flat slippers, and her face as nature made it, with the addition of the large round spectacles she wore for reading and knitting.

Hilary hooted. 'I'm not sure I meant you to go as far as that! Did he turn tail and zoom away in Edna?'

'No. He followed me into the house in a daze, then sat watching me open-mouthed as I put the beef and Yorkshire pudding on the table. Then,' said Candida, with a dramatic pause, 'he started to laugh. He laughed until he cried, then he tasted the first mouthful, after which he said nothing at all until he'd cleared his plate—twice.'

'So what happened then?'

'He took my glasses off after dinner, breathed "God, but you're beautiful" in the most chronic B-movie way and went off into gales of laughter again and—and took me off to bed. Where we stayed until next morning.'

'And?'

'We're getting married in six weeks' time. Jack says he won't wait a minute longer. He's in love with my gravy.'

Hilary laughed with Candida and gave her sincere congratulations, promised to be a bridesmaid, then gave in to a few bitter tears after she'd rung off.

'Fancy your sister marrying John Wynne Jones,' said Olwen next day at the library. 'He's so good-looking, I love his films. By the way, isn't he some sort of relative of Rhodri Lloyd-Ellis?'

'I believe he is. Second cousin or something,' said Hilary casually, and went off to help a schoolboy find the reference book he needed.

After a while Hilary stopped waiting for Rhodri to ring. But it was less easy to stop thinking about him. The days, even the evenings, weren't so bad. But at night her mind ran riot, with a tendency to dwell on the episode at the farm far too often for restful nights, wondering if those few fleeting moments were the nearest she was ever to come to knowing the bliss Candida had talked about. It seemed depressingly likely. Unless she managed to meet someone else. With this in view she gave in to Catrin's coaxing and joined the tennis club, which was a flourishing concern in Penafon, and, according to Catrin, a likely place to encounter the opposite sex because it had squash courts, and overlooked the cricket pitch.

'Which, now that summer isn't so far away, is a perfectly splendid idea,' said Catrin with satisfaction. 'Besides, I need some exercise after parking my rear end on an office chair all day long.'

Hilary was in full agreement, and as the evenings grew longer enjoyed two or three sets of tennis during the week, and as many as possible at the weekend. Life grew more supportable. She appreciated the company of the other members of the club, some of whom were young, male and unattached, and Penafon itself grew more lively, as tourists came to explore its attractions once the weather grew warmer. Hilary was doing very nicely, in her own opinion. Then, one evening, as she came running up her spiral stair, flushed from a particularly hard game of tennis, she could hear the telephone ringing. It stopped just as she reached it and she made a face at it. Candida probably, with the latest details of the wedding plans, warning her not to get too freckled for the great day.

Hilary went off to shower, but had to cut it short, wrapping herself in a towel as the telephone rang again.

'Hello, Hilary,' said Rhodri.

Hilary stood turned to stone, appalled to find she was shaking all over at the mere sound of his voice. 'Hello,' she said evenly. 'Who is this?'

'Rhodri. Rhodri Lloyd-Ellis, in case you've forgotten.' His tone was caustic, and the blood in Hilary's veins began to flow normally again.

'What a surprise. How are you?' she asked, rubbing at her hair with her free hand.

'Fairish. Are you well?'

'Very. I've just come in from playing tennis. I was in the shower when you rang.'

There was silence for a moment or two. 'That conjures up a very tempting picture in my mind, Hilary.'

She made no reply, her mouth tightening as she heard him sigh.

'Jack tells me there's a wedding in the offing soon,' Rhodri went on.

'Yes.'

'Are you pleased?'

'Of course I'm pleased.'

'I gather you're to be bridesmaid.'

'Yes.'

'Jack's asked me to be best man.'

'Oh.' Hilary sat down suddenly on the floor. For some reason that possibility hadn't even occurred to her.

'Do you mind?'

'No. No, I don't mind,' she murmured.

'Because if you do I can easily plead a business trip at the requisite time.'

'Unnecessary. I haven't done *much* growing up since we last met, of course, but enough, I think, not to cast a blight on my sister's wedding just because the best man and I don't see eye to eye.'

He laughed a little. Not the happiest of sounds, Hilary thought with a shiver.

'Very true,' said Rhodri. 'I'd have to lift you up to make it possible. Not that I wouldn't enjoy that enormously. Or all the other things we could do if you were in my arms.'

'I'd rather you didn't say things like that,' said Hilary sharply. 'Now, if you don't mind, I'd like to get dressed——' She stopped, biting her lip as another deliberate sigh greeted her words.

'I'd rather you didn't say things like *that*, either,' he said huskily. 'It's very bad for the blood pressure in one of my advancing years.'

'How inconvenient for you,' said Hilary blandly. 'Did I tell you I'd joined the tennis club, by the way? And I'm learning to play squash and badminton, and I've been asked to join the operatic society——'

'In fact, your life is full,' interrupted Rhodri, interpreting her words correctly.

'Busy, certainly. And I'm planning to become an Associate, too, which means writing papers and so on and doing quite a lot of studying——'

'In short, you're doing very nicely without my help.'

'Something like that. Not that I'm not grateful for your help, Rhodri. Believe me, I am. If you hadn't given me a lecture about growing up I imagine I'd still be mooning over you, imagining myself in love instead of getting on with my life.' Hilary waited, heart thumping, for his response, which was slow in coming.

'You don't need a hockey-stick to hit a man where it hurts, Hilary,' he said drily. 'However, since this is apparently the night for the whole truth and nothing but, I'd like you to know I was merely comforting Candida that day because she had the blues about Jack.'

'Of course you were. But I'm sure it was no hardship!' Hilary laughed a little. 'Anyway it all came right in the end. If Jack hadn't caught you *in flagrante*, as it were, he and Candida would probably still be shilly-shallying about.'

'There was no *flagrante* about it at all,' said Rhodri swiftly. 'What the hell do you think I am, Hilary?'

'Just a figure of speech, Rhodri!'

'I assure you that seduction was the last thing on my mind. I found someone in tears, so I did what anyone else would have done. To be brutally honest, if there was any seducing to be done, *you* were the one in danger from me, my child, not Candida. And just for the record, I don't go round poaching on other men's preserves. Like Jack's, for instance.'

'I see,' said Hilary soberly, rather overcome by the severity of the little lecture.

'I hope you do,' he said stringently, then to her relief he chuckled. 'Actually, Jack came after me that day looking pretty ominous. I was, he made it clear, never to lay a finger on either Candida or Edna again, which floored me completely, until I remembered Edna was that showy car of his.'

'When it comes to showy cars you can hardly throw stones,' Hilary pointed out.

'True. Pretty depressing, really. I see I've fallen completely from grace as far as you're concerned, Hilary.'

'Nonsense. And even if you have, I doubt you'll lose much sleep over it,' she retorted. 'Nevertheless, thank you for ringing, Rhodri. It was a nice thought, but don't worry. If Jack has forgiven you sufficiently to want you as best man, who am I to object? See you in church. Goodnight.'

CHAPTER TEN

HILARY stood very still in the aisle of the old Norman church at Iffley, her eyes misty as they rested on her sister. Candida looked so beautiful that there wasn't a dry eye on the bride's side of the church. A ray of sunlight struck sparks of gold from Candida's hair, even through the froth of veiling that covered it, and the rapt, radiant smile she'd given her waiting bridegroom on her arrival, had sent a sigh rippling through the congregation like a breeze through a cornfield. Hilary felt a lump in her throat as she saw the look on Jack's face as he slid the ring on Candida's finger, and looked away hastily, noting the pride on her father's tanned face, and the rather set look on her mother's beneath the big blue hat, which meant she was trying not to cry.

Why did people always cry at weddings? thought Hilary, and smiled a little, flushing as she looked up to meet Rhodri's eyes. Like Jack, he looked utterly magnificent in the formal grey morning suit, and several feminine eyes, particularly among the sprinkling of theatre friends on Jack's side, were eyeing the best man with speculation.

'Those whom God hath joined together let no man put asunder,' intoned the clergyman, and tightened his stole round the joined hands of bride and groom. The sapphire-blue eyes of the bride looked up, suddenly startled, into the glowing dark ones of her groom, who smiled in such tender reassurance that another sigh whispered through the people gathered together to see the actor take a wife.

Hilary took a grip on the flowers she carried, both her own delicate spray of gardenias and stephanotis, and the almost identical one Candida had chosen for herself. Gardenias were Candida's favourites, and they were everywhere, in the men's lapels, in Hilary's upswept hair, and in the floral displays decorating the church. No doubt, thought Hilary, with a pang, Rhodri had made sure they would be all over the place at the reception afterwards, too. As the ceremony came to a close she was swept along with the wedding party to the vestry, on a tide of kisses and congratulations, while the register was signed. Jack's parents, a lively, dark-haired pair with a similar sense of humour, teased their son as he seized Hilary and gave her an enthusiastic kiss.

'No more of that from now on, mind,' warned Huw Wynne Jones with a wink. 'Black eyes for you if Candida here catches you kissing anyone —except professionally, of course!'

'With a wife like mine, am I likely to?' demanded Jack, giving his bride a look which brought hectic colour to her face, and a concerted murmur of agreement from the others. 'Besides,' he added, 'the girl not only looks like an angel, she cooks like one into the bargain. What more can a man ask?'

'Have *you* learned how to cook yet?' murmured Rhodri in Hilary's ear.

'No,' she said shortly. 'I'm beaten on both points.'

'Come on, Rhodri,' urged Kate Wynne Jones. 'You've kissed the bride, but I didn't see you kiss the bridesmaid. You're slipping—lovely girl like that!'

'Easily remedied,' said Rhodri promptly, and took Hilary in his arms, flowers and all, and kissed her so thoroughly that she was hot and flustered by the time he released her to follow the bride and groom down the aisle.

'That was a bit unnecessary!' she muttered through stiff, smiling lips, as they posed for photographs outside the church.

'*I* liked it,' he said, from the corner of his mouth, then took her aside as the photographer arranged parents and relations in varied groups with the bride. The Press was there in force, and while Candida and Jack submitted to countless photographs from a barrage of cameras Rhodri kept a hand in the crook of Hilary's arm, as he pointed out the superb carvings round the west door of the old church.

'How lovely you look, Hilary,' he said softly, and gestured towards a particular detail, as though architecture were the subject under discussion.

'Thank you.' Hilary knew quite well that she'd never looked better, in the pale, muted gold of the plain silk dress Candida's unerring eye had chosen as the best foil for Hilary's tanned skin and sun-streaked brown hair. 'We'd better join the others.'

'Not yet. Your parents are getting on with Jack's like a house on fire, so stay here for a moment before we say "cheese" again for the final photograph.'

Hilary did as he said reluctantly, dismayed to find the touch of Rhodri's hand on her arm adding to the general assault on her emotions begun by the moving ritual of the wedding service. 'It was kind of you to offer your house for the reception,' she said with formality.

'Not in the least. Since Candida hated the idea of a stiff hotel reception, and your parents no longer have a home in this country, it seemed the best solution.' He smiled down at her. 'Even though I suspect you dislike my house.'

Hilary turned startled eyes up to him. 'I don't——' She caught her mother's eye, and detached herself quickly. 'Black your face—we're on. Time to smile for the birdie.'

Then they were caught up in the fray again as wedding guests surged round the wedding party and chased the bride and groom outside to the waiting Rolls, where they could shower them with confetti and rice once away from the church.

'Heavens,' said Anne Mason, once her husband had settled her safely in the car for the journey back to the reception. 'That was lively. It was a beautiful wedding, don't you think?'

'Certainly was, darling,' agreed Tom Mason, and grinned at Hilary. 'A bit of a relief, I must say. Thought we'd never get the girl off our hands.'

'Dad!' Hilary protested, and Rhodri, perched on a folding seat opposite her, shook his head and laughed.

'With daughters as beautiful as yours I can't believe that problem's caused you much concern, sir.'

Mrs Mason regarded at him with interest. 'Ah, but Hilary doesn't think she's even attractive, you know.'

'Which, of course,' said Rhodri, turning to look at Hilary, 'is utter nonsense.'

'Would you mind not discussing me as though I weren't here?' said Hilary crossly. 'Besides, this is Candida's day. Not mine.'

'Ah, but your day will come,' said Rhodri casually.

'But not for a long time yet,' she said with emphasis, and grinned at her father. 'Don't worry, Dad. I'll give you plenty of time to save up. Years and years at the very least.'

The wedding breakfast was a happy, high-spirited affair, all the main ground-floor rooms of Rhodri's house thronged with Wynne Jones relatives happy to see each other, and eager to mix with Jack's actor friends, at the same time making sure that the rather quieter Mason contingent participated to the full in the fun.

'Hilly!' called a familiar voice, and Hilary turned away from conversation with one of the consultants Candida worked for to see a radiant fair girl with a tall, red-headed man in tow.

'Davy Lennox!' said Hilary, then laughed in apology. 'Oops, sorry—Davy Seymour now, isn't it?'

'You bet it is!' the man emphatically, and slid his arm round his wife. 'I'm Leo Seymour, and you're Candida's little sister.'

'All grown up now, though,' said Davina admiringly, 'and very nicely, too.'

'How do you do?' said Hilary to Leo, her eyes drawn to the tent-like silk dress the other girl was wearing. 'I say, Davy, are you——?'

'Certainly am,' said Davina Seymour, smiling up at her husband. 'A new little Seymour's expected in October. We've asked Candida and Jack to be godparents.'

'Wonderful—congratulations!' Hilary gave Davy a kiss, then caught her mother's eye. 'Sorry, must dash, it's speech-time. I hope Dad doesn't muff it.'

All the speeches went off well, as was to be expected, with an actor as the star turn. Rhodri's speech was smooth and brief, and included a graceful tribute to Hilary, and afterwards Candida made for the stairs on her way to change. As she reached the landing she smiled down at the upturned faces then tossed her bouquet high in the air in a wide arc. Hilary dodged away, but there was a great roar of laughter as Rhodri reached up a negligent hand and caught the flowers, then turned and presented them to the sister of the bride with a bow. Jack clapped Rhodri on the shoulder, then sprinted upstairs after his bride, smiling wickedly over his shoulder and saying, 'Don't worry, Mam, we're in separate rooms, I promise. For now, anyway!'

Nell, Candida's room-mate, sighed enviously beside Hilary. 'You're sister's terribly lucky, Hilly. What a man!'

'He's not doing so badly in return!' said Hilary promptly, and looked round embarrassed as Rhodri laughed softly behind her.

'Always your sister's champion!'

'As if Candida needed one,' said Nell ruefully, 'with all she's got going for her!'

When the deliriously happy pair had been waved off by the assembled guests the party began to break up. Jack had vetoed any evening celebrations and was whisking his bride straight off to a medieval farmhouse in the Périgord in France for the week he was being allowed off from the play, and, as always at weddings, those left behind felt a little flat as the wedding guests drifted gradually away, leaving only a nucleus of family. Hilary, in particular, felt doubly bereft, since Rhodri had insisted on driving Candida and Jack to Heathrow himself, and the house seemed melancholy as the caterers cleared away the debris of the wedding feast.

'Let's sort out the presents people actually brought with them today,' said Kate Wynne Jones, and Anne Mason brightened, happy to have something to do. Hilary joined in, her silken splendour exchanged now for a new cotton dress her mother had bought her.

'I hope they've got room for all this stuff in that poky London flat of Jack's,' said his mother, shaking her head.

'Don't worry,' said Hilary, grinning. 'I don't think they'll be there long. Candida wants somewhere in the country she can fill with children and dogs and muddy rubber boots. Jack will just have to commute.'

'Or get a proper job!' said his father, to everyone's amusement. 'Now then, Tom, it's settled that you and Anne are coming to dinner with us at the hotel tonight, so I think it's time we made a move. How about you, young Hilary? Are you going to grace us old ones with your company?'

Before Hilary could say yes, her mother intervened casually. 'Actually, Hilly, would you mind hanging on to see the caterers off? And I think someone ought to be here when Rhodri gets back.'

'Good idea, *cariad*,' said Kate Wynne Jones, understanding perfectly. 'Come on, you two men. Hilary can cope with the rest of this stuff.'

By the time Rhodri Lloyd-Ellis returned from the airport his house was tidy and deserted, except for a stack of re-crated wedding presents in his dining-room, and a rather forlorn, awkward girl who came into the hall as he let himself in, looking as though she'd rather be anywhere in the world but where she was.

'Hello,' Hilary said in a small voice. 'Mother thought I should wait until you got back. To say thank you and all that, and how very grateful she is to you. For lending your house, I mean.'

'My pleasure,' he said, yawning. 'Sorry. Heavy night last night with Jack, and a bit of a wait at the airport. The plane had a spot of engine trouble which had to be put right before they could take off.'

'Oh. That's why you were so long. I thought——' She stopped, flushing.

Rhodri ushered her into his study, eyeing her closely as she passed. 'Did you think I'd had an accident, Hilary?'

'The thought did occur to me.'

'I had only half a glass of champagne, you know!'

'I noticed.'

He smiled. 'Then, since we seem to be in sole possession of a brace of bottles I purposely put to one side, I vote we toast the bride and groom in peace all on our own now I'm at liberty to enjoy my champagne.'

'Lovely,' she said, and meant it.

'While I rustle up the wine, would you switch on the television? I might catch the last of the one-day Test.'

Hilary did as he said, and settled down to watch the last overs of the day with Rhodri, amused at his absorption, even flattered by it in a way, as though they were old friends, and comfortable in each other's company. She curled up in her chair, feeling weary. Weddings, she decided, were tiring.

The cricket finally came to a close, with a win for England, which pleased Rhodri because one of the Glamorgan bowlers was included in the team, he informed Hilary.

She laughed. 'Of course. I'm sure England would never have managed it without help from one of you Welsh!'

Rhodri smiled, and refilled her glass. 'Hungry, by the way?'

'Not in the least. A bit tired, in fact.'

'Shall we just sit here for a while, then?' he suggested. 'This programme about sailing only lasts for half an hour or so.'

Hilary was quite happy to stay where she was indefinitely, chatting desultorily as Rhodri explained the intricacies of dinghy sailing to her, then as the programme ended they both shot bolt upright, as the newscast which followed it included an item about an aircrash in its headline. Rhodri got to his feet, suddenly tense, as the newsreader informed them a plane from Heathrow had crashed on landing at Nice Airport, giving the flight number, and a phone number to ring for the information. Without a word Rhodri ran from the room and began dialling the number, the expression on his face making questions superfluous.

Clenching her teeth to keep them from chattering like castanets, Hilary moved close to him. He reached out an arm and pulled her against him as he dialled the emergency number over and over again until he got through. Her ribs felt as though they would crack as Rhodri held her cruelly close, but Hilary was glad of the pain, which helped stifle the panic threatening to get out of control inside her. Surely fate couldn't be so cruel!

'Are there survivors?' she asked, her voice cracking as she put her fear into words.

Rhodri put a finger to his lips, listening intently to the voice which answered his questions, then expressed his thanks fervently and put the receiver down, seizing Hilary in his arms and rubbing his cheek hard against hers. 'The plane failed to stop on the runway,' he said unsteadily, 'but, thank goodness, it didn't catch fire. There was no one killed, but several people injured slightly. The Press over there had got wind of the wedding and were hanging about for Jack and his new bride, luckily, so it was quickly established they were unhurt—don't cry, darling, they're safe.' And Rhodri turned Hilary's suddenly drenched face up to his and kissed her in a fever of relief and thanksgiving.

'*Oh!*—my parents!' said Hilary, dragging her mouth away. 'Rhodri they'll be at the hotel, they might hear accidentally—— '

'I'll get through to the Randolph right now.'

And in minutes Hilary was speaking to both her own father and Jack's, to give them the news, Rhodri relieving her of the receiver half-way through to add his confirmation that all was well, and to advise them to stay where they were, since Jack was certain to get in touch with them at the hotel as soon as he could.

Hilary was shivering, her teeth chattering with shock when Rhodri put down the telephone, and he hurried her into the big kitchen, insisting she sat down at the table while he made her strong black coffee, heavily sugared, to counteract the shock. He added a shot of brandy to it for good measure.

'Right. Drink this quickly,' he ordered, and stood over her while she swallowed it down, then they both ran for the hall as the telephone rang.

'Hello,' barked Rhodri, then he relaxed. 'Candida! Heavens you gave us a fright—hang on, here's Hilary.'

'Candida!' cried Hilary hoarsely. 'Are you sure you're all right?'

Candida gave emphatic assurances that, apart from shock, both she and Jack were fine, but if she had any say in the matter the journey home would be made by road. She said that Jack had rung his parents at the Randolph and found the Masons were there too, which had killed two birds with one stone, a phrase which made Hilary shudder. Now he was waiting at his bride's elbow to get on with their honeymoon. Candida gave a little squeak, and could be heard scolding her husband, who took over the phone and added his reassurances that all was well.

'You know what actors are like, Hilary,' he said outrageously. 'Anything for publicity!'

Hilary called him a very unladylike name, handed Rhodri over for a moment or two, then subsided limply on the settle, feeling so shattered it was an effort to speak to her mother when the phone rang again the moment Rhodri put it down. Her parents were anxious to know whether Hilary was all right, and if she wanted them to get back to Candida's house at once.

'Since at the moment I'm not there, no, Mother. You enjoy your dinner now the excitement's over.' She looked up at Rhodri uncertainly, and he took the receiver from her yet again.

'Don't worry, Mrs Mason,' he said soothingly. 'I'll bring Hilary back safely later on.'

'I'm afraid you rather got stuck with me,' said Hilary, when they went back to the kitchen.

'Which is exactly what I wanted.' He grinned, and opened the refrigerator. 'But under the circumstances I hope you don't mind if I cook you a meal here, because frankly I just don't fancy trekking into town to Le Petit Blanc, as originally intended. We'll save that for some other time.'

'I don't remember being asked to Le Petit Blanc,' said Hilary sharply.

'I asked your mother if she'd mind if I whisked you off for the evening, intending to spring it on you as a surprise later, when I took you into town. Unfortunately events rather overtook us, didn't they?' Rhodri yawned widely.

'You sound as though you'd do better to go to bed,' said Hilary, then flushed as he gave her a very straight look.

'Funny you should say that. I couldn't help thinking about that in church as I watched the ceremony,' he said huskily. 'Odd, really, because I'm sure Candida and Jack are lovers already anyway. But the marriage ceremony makes a difference somehow, doesn't it? Lifts the whole thing into a different sphere.'

'They also happen to be very much in love with each other.' Hilary leaned her chin in her hands. 'Incidentally, it probably did Candida a power of good today to see Davy Seymour looking quite definitely pregnant.'

Rhodri looked blank. 'Why?'

'Because it must be pretty difficult for Jack to harbour any romantic ideas about a lost love when the love in question is as big as a house and obviously pleased as Punch about it.'

'And in the case of Davina Seymour has a very possessive husband to add to the score.' Rhodri shrugged. 'Besides, once Jack started seeing something of Candida I think he forgot any languishing about Davina. His main worry was that he was just one of a crowd as far as Candida was concerned.'

'The only one she's ever wanted.' Hilary smiled. 'Good thing you precipitated matters by making him jealous.'

'In one way.' Rhodri stared at her gloomily. 'But it did me a whole lot of no good as far as you were concerned. For the second time in our very brief relationship you more or less told me to get lost.'

'But that wasn't over Candida!'

His eyes narrowed. 'No?'

'No fear,' she assured him. 'It was your spiel about my need to grow up. I—took exception to it.'

'I see.' Rhodri was silent for a while, looking at Hilary very thoughtfully.

'I feel like something under a microscope,' she informed him tartly.

'Sorry. I was thinking. Look, Hilary, can't we call it quits and start from the beginning again?'

'No.' She got up briskly to inspect the contents of the refrigerator. 'If you'll settle for cold chicken and salad I think I could manage to rustle it up without too much difficulty.'

'How do you expect me to eat when you've just turned me down flat, woman?' he demanded wrathfully.

'I haven't. I just said I didn't want to go back to the beginning again. I vote we just go on from here.'

CHAPTER ELEVEN

RHODRI demanded clarification, and since neither of them was over-hungry Hilary put together a plate of chicken sandwiches while she made her position clear.

'I'd really like us to be friends, Rhodri,' she said honestly. 'If you feel the same perhaps you'd care to take me out for a meal or something now and then, when you're in my neighbourhood, and give me a ring occasionally. But only if you want to, of course. In the meantime I go on with the life I've made for myself in Penafon, and if, eventually, I manage to grow up sufficiently to please you, fine. If I don't, no harm done, and we'll stay friends, which will be a lot more convenient than downright enemies. After all,' she added with a mischievous grin, 'we're relatives now, you know, in a tenuous sort of way!'

Rhodri ran a hand through his thick, waving hair, looking rather dampened. 'It all sounds very clinical, put like that. Am I to take it that this—friendship of ours excludes any physical expressions of affection?'

'You mean kissing and so on?'

'You know damn well I do!'

Hilary frowned. 'I'm not sure that's a good idea. So far, when you've made love to me it simplifies things to a much too dangerous extent.'

Rhodri refilled her champagne glass. 'In what way?' he asked, brightening.

'When you kiss me I, personally, don't care a damn whether I've grown up enough for you or not,' said

Hilary bluntly. 'Back at the ranch there I would have been all for it if you'd gone a lot further than kissing. Which is worrying. So until I've made up your mind as to whether I'll do or not, I think we'd better rule out lovemaking.' She watched his reaction closely, glee bubbling up inside her at the rather nettled look on his face.

'What the hell do you mean—"whether you'll do"?' he demanded irritably. 'You are a very attractive, intelligent, but frighteningly innocent creature, Hilary, and I merely think you should learn a bit more about the world in actual fact rather than in books, before——'

'Before what, Rhodri?' she asked curiously.

'Before committing yourself in any way,' he said without inflection.

'You mean I should have a few lovers——'

'No, I bloody well do not!' he said explosively, and jumped up to pour the rest of the champagne into their glasses. 'I meant you should get to know more men as *friends*——'

'Rhodri, I haven't exactly been in a nunnery since I left school,' she pointed out. 'I went to college, remember. There were plenty of males hanging about there, I assure you. Young ones like me, of course, which is probably the trouble. I didn't have the good fortune to encounter anyone sophisticated like you to polish my rough edges and so on.'

Hilary rather fancied she could hear Rhodri grinding his teeth, and sipped her champagne with relish.

'Hilary,' he said, with exaggerated patience. 'I think you've misunderstood me somewhere along the line.'

'Really?'

'Don't look at me like that,' he growled. 'Those blue eyes of yours will get you into trouble one day. I thought you'd learnt that already with Probert.'

'You turned out to be far more of a threat than Rhys Probert!' she said tartly.

He stared at her, frustrated, then swallowed the contents of his glass and set it down on a table with a force that almost cracked it.

'All right, Hilary,' he said. 'I'll now call a taxi and put you in it and send you back safe and sound to your parents. And in the morning I'll come round at about eleven and take you out to lunch before you start back to Penafon. When do your parents go back to Portugal?'

'Next weekend. They're coming back with me to Penafon and putting up at the Afon Arms until then. Mother wants to make sure my flat and its surroundings are respectable enough to meet with her approval.'

'Naturally. I know how she feels.' Without warning Rhodri pulled her to her feet and into his arms and looked down into her startled face. 'To sum up, Hilary, I shall do exactly as you suggest for a period of three months. If, at the end of that time, either of us wishes to terminate the arrangement we must let the other one know.'

'Gosh!' breathed Hilary. 'How businesslike!'

He ignored her. 'However, since, as I've pointed out before, I do happen to be a poor hapless male, I think I merit one kiss before we embark on this admirably platonic course of action. Are you in agreement?'

She nodded reluctantly and raised her face, eyes closed, for the kiss. Nothing happened. Hilary opened her eyes again, to see Rhodri watching her with a caustic gleam in his eye.

'If it's that much of a sacrifice,' he informed her, 'I don't think I'll call on you to make it.'

'Oh, for heaven's sake come here,' she said impatiently, and reached up to pull his head down to hers so she could kiss the sarcastic smile away from his mouth. As their lips met both of them forgot the skirmishing of the previous minutes. The kiss Rhodri asked for went on for so long that both of them were breathing hard when they separated at last.

'I want more than that,' he said unsteadily. 'Would it contravene regulations very badly to let me kiss you back?'

Hilary merely buried her head against his chest, and Rhodri picked her up and sat down with her in his lap, his tongue probing delicately at her lips until they opened so generously to him that he gave a smothered sound of satisfaction deep in his throat. Hilary curled closer, her hands locked about his neck as she returned his kisses, her earlier veto on lovemaking forgotten in the heat and delight of the moment. It was only a matter of seconds before kisses were no longer enough. Their hands smoothed and caressed each other's bodies with mounting urgency through the thin cotton of her dress and his shirt, then his long fingers slid into her hair, removing the hairpins from her expensively constructed knot, until her curls tumbled about her face and neck and he could bury his face against their fragrance.

The doorbell brought them back to earth with a jolt. They both jumped to their feet, exchanging looks of consternation, then Rhodri tucked in his shirt hastily on his way to answer the door while Hilary rummaged in her handbag for a comb to repair some of the havoc Rhodri's hands had created. The sound of her parents' voices gave her such a guilty pang of dismay it was an effort to summon up the smile of welcome she gave her father and mother as Rhodri ushered them into the room.

'No, we won't stop for coffee,' said Anne Mason, in response to Rhodri's offer. 'The taxi's waiting outside, and we thought Hilary might be a bit tired after all the excitement, so we'll take her off your hands and get her to bed. It's been quite a day!'

Saved by the bell, thought Hilary, turning away hurriedly from the look in Rhodri's eye, which told her plainly that he was thinking the same thing. There was a flurry of goodnights, and no opportunity for anything more than repeated thanks to Rhodri for his share of the day's celebrations before Hilary was borne off with her parents, suffering badly from a sense of anticlimax.

It was a feeling she learnt to live with, because, rather to her surprise in the circumstances, Rhodri was true to his word. As the summer went on he obeyed Hilary's edict to the letter. He rang her regularly, sent her postcards when his job took him abroad, and came to Penafon every so often to take her out for a meal, always returning her punctiliously early to her flat afterwards, and never taking her up on her offer of coffee or a drink before he went off to stay the night in the room permanently reserved for him at Cwmderwen Court Hotel.

To Hilary's secret regret Rhodri never made any attempt to initiate any form of physical contact beyond that necessary to help her into the car, or hold out her chair for her at the dinner-table in the places where he wined and dined her. Instead they discussed books and television plays and some of the deals Rhodri was involved in, and whether the guest-room at his house in Oxford should have its walls painted blue or white.

'What's going on?' demanded Candida. 'Just how pally *are* you two?'

'Just good friends,' Hilary assured her. Which was the absolute truth. No relationship could have been more platonic. 'How's the blushing bride?'

Not that there was need to ask. Candida was only too happy to extol the bliss of being married to Jack, and went on at such length that Hilary was almost sorry she'd asked.

In some ways Hilary was glad of the arrangement she had forced on Rhodri as a sort of test of his intentions to her, feeling it would at least tell her whether he was genuinely interested in her, or whether a mere long-distance friendship would pall after a while. In the meantime she got on with both her jobs, and put money away for the air fare to Portugal and the holiday she intended enjoying with her parents the following spring. She was fired with an ambition to see the almond-blossom in bloom in the Algarve, which was now a viable proposition with the aid of her extra income from Redman's.

Catrin was frankly intrigued by Rhodri's regular appearance in Penafon. 'Just good friends, eh?' she said knowingly. 'Well, if you say so, *cariad*, but it seems strange to me. If I were seeing Rhodri Lloyd-Ellis every now and then—and don't tell me he comes up this way for any other reason, my girl—I think I'd be more than "just friends" by now.'

Hilary smiled serenely and said no more, and went on playing tennis and badminton, and helping with cricket teas when the local team played at home. As she informed Rhodri on one occasion, he could hardly say she wasn't meeting enough men. His answering smile was bland, as he advised her to stick to the unattached ones if she were sensible, but there was a calculating gleam in his eye as he handed over a new historical bestseller he'd brought her from London. As he knew quite well, this was more than enough to send thoughts of any cricketers straight out of Hilary's head.

Exactly three months to the day after Candida's wedding Rhodri suggested Hilary come to Oxford for the weekend. Jack and Candida would be there too, he told her, because Jack had just left the cast of his West End play to make a film for Leo Seymour again, and was having a short rest before Leo began shooting.

Hilary was filled with excitement at the prospect. After three months of blameless existence in Penafon, fond of the town though she was, it would be less than the truth to say she didn't welcome a change, cricket match or not. Someone else could butter the bread this time.

She set off as arranged on the Friday night, very pleased with life. The evening was sunny, she had a Saturday off from the library, and she loved Oxford anyway, Rhodri's presence or not. All in all, she decided, it was good to be alive, and she sang along with the radio as she drove at her usual conservative pace, her pulse quickening when at last she drew up a little way from Rhodri's house in the quiet road on the northern outskirts of the university city.

Hilary gave herself a minute for necessary repairs to her face and hair, also, she admitted, to compose herself a little before she came face to face with Rhodri for the first time in three weeks. He'd been away on the Continent on business, which meant their communication had been limited to a few unsatisfactory telephone calls and the odd postcard, and she'd missed him badly. Hilary could hardly contain her joy at the thought of seeing him again, and her heart leapt as the tall gates opened and he came running towards her, smiling that eye-crinkling smile of his as he relieved her of her suitcase.

He looked lean and fit, and, in shirt and trousers of the same cream linen, his eyes glittering like crystal in his tanned face, he was more attractive than a man had a right to look, to Hilary's prejudiced eyes.

'Hilary, how are you?' he said and hurried her into the house. 'I never make allowances for the speed, or lack of it, of that old heap of yours. I was beginning to worry—even rang your flat to see if you'd left.'

Hilary laughed, secretly very much elated by his concern. 'I never arrive anywhere without getting a scolding for taking so long! But I'm here now, and I've got a terrific thirst, and I'm starving!'

Chattering away nineteen to the dozen, Hilary followed Rhodri to the kitchen, where a cold supper was awaiting. 'When do Candida and Jack arrive?' she asked eagerly after a while.

'Later. They said to start without them, so let's eat out here, shall we?'

Hilary nodded happily, only too ready to fall on the food, which Rhodri informed her his Mrs Bray had left ready for him.

'You're spoilt,' she informed him, as she tasted the seafood salad. 'This is wonderful.'

He laughed, and poured wine into her glass. 'Try some of this, it's not too dry, I promise.'

'You always remember!'

'Yes,' he said lightly. 'I remember most things you've said to me over the months.'

'Very flattering.'

'You look quite lovely tonight, Hilary,' he said, gazing at her instead of getting on with his meal. 'You literally glow.'

'It's all the tennis and virtuous living,' she assured him. 'Marvellous for the skin. I've been dieting too. Do you think I've lost weight?'

'I hope not. I liked you as you were.'

Hilary looked at him over her glass. 'Don't you like me as I am now? Or is that question not allowable now I've grown up a bit more?' She gave him a dry look. 'I shall be twenty-one next January, you know.'

'I do know. Beginning of Hilary Term.'

Hilary began to feel a little restive under the intent grey stare, which seemed even more brilliant tonight than usual, and for the rest of the meal she plunged into questions about Rhodri's travels, finding she was less hungry than she thought in the face of his diamond-bright scrutiny. She refused offers of pudding or cheese, and agreed that coffee in the study would be lovely, pleased he didn't expect them to wait in the rather formal splendour of the drawing-room until the others arrived.

She excused herself to visit the bathroom, and took some time to tidy herself up, examining herself critically in the mirror, rather taken aback to see herself so flushed, her eyes glowing like lamps in a face as tanned as Rhodri's. She tucked her blue silk shirt into the new trousers which fitted so perfectly, ran a comb through her hair and glanced at her watch. Almost ten. Candida was late, which was unusual. She had strong views on punctuality, but since nowadays these were probably affected by Jack, Hilary saw no point in worrying quite yet.

When she returned downstairs Rhodri had some Ravel playing in the background, and a tray of coffee, flanked by a brandy decanter and a bottle of Grand Marnier, waited on a low table near the sofa.

'Which would you like?' he asked.

Hilary hesitated. Normally she drank very little other than a glass of wine, but tonight she found she quite welcomed the idea of a little Dutch courage. Which was

extraordinary. What on earth was there to be afraid of?
'I think I'd like some Grand Marnier, please.'

The combination of strong hot coffee and the fiery
orange taste of the liqueur was rather startling. Hilary
felt a glow start up inside her which added quickly to
the colour of her cheeks. Rhodri laughed as she fanned
herself with a record sleeve.

'Don't worry. The colour suits you. Makes your eyes
shine like jewels. I've always had a weakness for blue
eyes,' he added casually.

'Are Sarah's blue?' Damn, thought Hilary. What a
stupid thing to say.

'Yes. But very different. Keeping to jewels, I suppose
one could call hers turquoise, whereas yours are a very
dark sapphire.' Rhodri leaned over to top Hilary's liqueur
glass, smiling very directly into those same sapphire-blue
eyes in a way which prompted Hilary to down her drink
in one swallow, blinking as the spirit brought tears to
her eyes.

'Steady,' warned Rhodri, amused, and she smiled and
drank some coffee, which seemed to make matters worse.
She felt hotter than ever.

'Are you still in love with her?' she blurted, and sank
her teeth into her lower lip in dismay. What was the
matter with her? 'Sorry,' she added swiftly. 'Forget I
asked that. Please. Absolutely none of my business.'

Rhodri swirled the brandy round in the crystal glass
he held to the light. 'I don't know precisely what you've
heard about Sarah and me,' he said slowly. 'But I rather
fancy you've got the wrong end of the stick, you know.
I've had far more lasting relationships in the past with
other ladies.'

If he thought he was comforting her, he was on the
wrong tack, thought Hilary, and held out her liqueur

glass. 'Could I have some more, please? I rather like Grand Marnier. I've never had it before.'

'You don't knock it back like best bitter!' He hesitated, then shrugged and filled the tiny glass half-full. 'Since you're not driving anywhere, I suppose it doesn't matter all that much.'

'Thank you,' said Hilary solemnly, and sipped with more caution. That was better. A little at a time was less inflammatory. 'So why does everyone go on about your being engaged to Sarah Morgan, then, if you've been living with several others?'

Rhodri's eyebrows met forbiddingly. 'There weren't *that* many. Also, since you're in quizzical mood, the simple fact is that I've never cared enough for any one lady to share my life so intimately.'

'Except the divine Sarah!'

'Not quite the case, actually.' He looked at her for a moment, then shrugged again. 'In actual fact my engagement to Sarah lasted for only two days. Officially it was longer than that, of course, but eventually she married her present husband and no explanation was ever given for the switch.'

Hilary stared at him in astonishment. 'Two *days*? I don't understand.'

'She had a quarrel with her Rupert, rushed home to her sister's wedding without the mysterious fiancé she'd promised to produce, and met me on the train journey. I drove her home from Newport, and deposited her with her family, who assumed I was the fiancé in question. Being really a very nice sort of chap at heart I stepped in and said I was—even provided her with one of my mother's rings to make it look like the real thing. Then Rupert reappeared in hot pursuit and I wasn't needed any more. End of story.'

Hilary gazed at Rhodri's inscrutable face for some time in silence.

'If,' she began carefully, 'this Rupert person had *not* reappeared, would you have been happy to carry on with the engagement?'

'Yes, I think so. I'd known Sarah since she was a child, remember, so it was no chance acquaintance. On the other hand, I think it only fair to say that since Sarah was irrevocably in love with said Rupert I'm glad things went no further than they did. My heart didn't suffer permanent damage, whatever you may have heard.' He leaned forward and looked deep into her eyes. 'I'm not the type to sigh after any woman who makes it clear she has no interest in me.'

Hilary drank the rest of her liqueur, feeling very much happier. She smiled at him radiantly. 'I'm glad you're not still suffering from unrequited passion, Rhodri.'

'Ah,' he said with an unsettling smile. 'You may be wrong there, Hilary. For Sarah, who is a married lady with two small sons at the last count, I'm not fool enough to cherish any unrequited longings, believe me. Which doesn't mean I'm immune to similar feelings towards other members of your sex, of course.'

Hilary didn't like the sound of that. She looked uneasily at her watch. 'Shouldn't Candida and Jack be here by now?'

Rhodri gave her a look which made her heart thump. 'Confession time. They're not coming tonight. I invited them for tomorrow and Sunday.'

'Oh, but——' Hilary stopped, biting her lip. There had been no mention of the actual day of arrival. The weekend, Candida had said. Hilary had taken it for granted the others would be arriving tonight, like herself.

She jumped up angrily. 'Then I'll go and beg a bed from Nell——'

'No, Hilary.' Rhodri pressed her back in her seat with an inexorable hand. 'I want you to stay right where you are and listen to me. We agreed on a three-month trial period for this odd, ambiguous arrangement of ours, right?'

She nodded dumbly.

'And we said that this could be terminated by either of us if we tired of it?'

Hilary nodded again.

'So I simply invited you here a day early to thrash out what happens next. I put my case forward, then you either accept it or put forward an alternative of your own.'

'This isn't a tribunal, Rhodri,' she said miserably. 'This is just you and me. I thought we were friends!'

'We are. In some ways. Possibly all ways as far as you're concerned. But I'll make no bones about the fact that I'm bloody fed up with the present situation myself.' Rhodri smiled. 'Don't look like that. I'm not about to leap on you.'

'I didn't think you were.'

'All I mean is that I can't go on with this platonic relationship, my little friend. I happen to be made of flesh and blood. And I want you.' Rhodri held up a hand as her eyes flashed up at him in alarm. 'Hear me out, please. If you say to me now, "Rhodri, I can never be anything more to you than a friend," I promise you can go straight to bed in the guest-room I had painted blue, as you suggested, and I shan't lay a finger on you. On the other hand, if you say you, like me, yearn for something more like a man–woman relationship, I still shan't trouble you unless——'

'Unless what?' she whispered.

'Unless you ask me to—in words of one syllable, Hilary.' Rhodri's eyes narrowed to slivers of gleaming crystal as they held hers. 'Ever since the first memorable moment we met I seem to have had no peace. And I've come to the conclusion that I never will have unless you——' He hesitated, then said without inflection, 'Unless you show me proof of this new maturity of yours.'

The warmth from the Grand Marnier ebbed away. Hilary felt very sober as she looked at him with careful consideration. 'Proof?' she questioned.

Rhodri nodded gravely. 'It's been clear to me for some time that it's just not possible for us to be mere friends, Hilary. Somewhere along the way you seem to have got under my skin. You're independent, suspicious, prickly, and very young, Hilary Mason. But physically you're all woman. The fact that I'm sure you've never had a lover keeps me awake at nights because I so much want to be your first lover, the one who teaches you what physical love means. I am right, Hilary? You've never had a lover?'

First lover? Hilary eyed him blankly. Did he mean to be just first of a long list? All the glow of anticipation she had felt earlier vanished at his words, which hurt, badly. And made her deeply angry. The cold tide inside her began to turn, heating to boiling point as the temper she had latterly learned to control threatened to swamp her in a great scalding rush. She clenched her teeth instead of the fists which longed to box Rhodri's ears, and turned away.

'You're very quiet, Hilary,' he said, sounding strained.

Only because I'm too choked by hurt and fury to answer, she thought, and took a firm grip of her emotions as she swung to face him again. He scanned her face questioningly.

'Surely you have something to say?'

'Yes,' she said levelly. 'I do.' As she spoke a course of action crystallised in Hilary's mind. 'You are, of course, quite right. I've never had a lover. Yet. In which case, since you mentioned the subject of my youth—relative though it is—I find I'm nervous. Perhaps if I'd known what you had in mind for tonight I'd have been more prepared for the idea.'

'I shouldn't have discussed it,' said Rhodri, sounding bitter. 'I was a fool. I should have kissed you senseless, then carried up up to bed. *My* bed.'

Hilary nodded calmly. 'Yes. Discussing it all before-hand was not one of your better ideas.' She gave him a collected little smile. 'But since we have, I'd like to think it over, please—in your spare-room.'

He stood rubbing his chin, his mouth set, then shrugged. 'So be it. Do I take it you'll let me know how you feel tomorrow, before the others arrive?'

'Oh, yes,' she assured him, and gave him a glittering smile. 'First thing in the morning, you'll know at once what I've decided.'

Rhodri shook his head, a very wry twist to his mobile mouth. 'All of which augurs badly for a good night's sleep on my part.'

Hilary hoped very much he was wrong. The room he showed her was charming, decorated in blue and gold and cream, with a deep-pile carpet almost the exact shade of her hair, she saw, as she looked in the mirror and saw the room reflected behind her. She made automatic preparations for the night and got into the comfortable bed to lie awake, listening for the sound of Rhodri's footsteps on the stairs. It seemed hours before he came to bed, and she tensed as she heard him pause outside her door. Her heart thumped so loudly she was sure he must be able to hear, and she lay, hardly daring to breathe, until she heard him move quietly away to the far end of the landing to his own room.

There had been many nights in her life when Hilary had slept badly, most of them since Rhodri's advent, but never before had she learnt what it meant to stay wide awake all night. Sleep was impossible as she thought of her high hopes as she'd driven here earlier, certain then that this weekend would be a turning-point in her life, the end of the silly three-month trial period, and the beginning of something else more enduring.

She shuddered in the summer darkness. How naïve she had been to imagine Rhodri intended asking her to marry him. His intentions had turned out to be insultingly different. It would hardly set the River Cherwell on fire, of course, if they were to become lovers. Most people did these days before settling down to a more permanent arrangement. Hilary flung herself over on to her back, staring at the white glimmer of the ceiling, knowing full well that as far as Rhodri Lloyd-Ellis was concerned she wanted everything, or nothing.

As the first faint glimmer of dawn crept into the room Hilary got up noiselessly and dressed, then crept down the stairs, her heart in her mouth until she reached the double glass inner doors in the square hall. She slipped the catch on the lock, blessing the well-run household which kept its locks and hinges oiled, then slid through into the small lobby and closed the doors behind her, relieved to find the outer doors opened just as easily. Within moments she was behind the wheel of her Mini and heading for Penafon.

Hilary drove along quiet, empty roads, numb with unhappiness and lack of sleep, wishing forlornly that she still had her old home in Warwickshire to run to, that she could shut herself up in the comfort of her childhood bedroom and cry and cry until she'd washed Rhodri Lloyd-Ellis out of her life for good. As it was 1A Glebe Row was the next best thing. Her getaway would spoil Candida's weekend, probably, but it couldn't be helped; there was no alternative. And from now on she would make very sure that all men stayed at arm's length until Miss Hilary Mason had learnt to be a lot less vulnerable, and a great deal better versed in the ways of the opposite sex.

It was still early when Hilary finally reached her goal. Penafon was just beginning to start its Saturday. Shops were pulling down striped blinds against the sun, and in Glebe Row the only curtains still drawn were Catrin's. Hilary eased her back wearily and locked the car, then climbed the iron stair on leaden feet. She unlocked her door and opened windows, filled the kettle, turned down her bed, then remembered her holdall was still in the car. She called herself a rude name and ran headlong back down the ironwork spiral, then screamed as she missed her footing half-way down and fell heavily the remainder of the way, landing on the pavement with a bruising thump, her foot doubled beneath her.

In a second the door of 1B flew open and Catrin hurtled through it in a dressing-gown, followed by Rhys Probert at top speed, quickly joined by several neighbours. For a few minutes pandemonium reigned, while Hilary, white and shaking with shock and pain, discovered that even with Rhys's help she couldn't stand on the foot she had landed on so awkwardly. Mrs Price from a couple of doors down ran inside to ring the

doctor, and Catrin flew ahead up to the flat to make tea
while her brother lifted Hilary in his powerful arms and
carried her as easily as a child straight to her bed, where
he let her down with care.

'Bloody stairs,' he said violently. 'I'll get them torn
down and replaced, if I have to use threats on Ned Lewis
to do it.'

The gentleman in question, Hilary's landlord, appeared at the door right on cue, full of distress over the
accident and promising to do something about the spiral
stair at once.

Catrin thrust a cup of tea in Hilary's hand and shooed
the arguing men away, her dark eyes bright with anxiety.
'There, love, drink this. You look ghastly.'

'I feel ghastly,' gasped Hilary. 'And hideously embarrassed. What a stupid, stupid thing to do.'

'What are you doing here, anyway? I thought you were
in Oxford.'

'I came back,' said Hilary, so bitterly that Catrin said
no more, sending Rhys down to the car for Hilary's bag
instead. And then the doctor arrived, and probed the
ankle, which stretched the patient's endurance to the
limit, but left her happier afterwards, since he diagnosed only a slight sprain, strapped it up, and advised
resting it for a few days.

'Thank goodness for that,' said Catrin. 'I thought you
might have broken it.' She helped Hilary undress,
sponged her perspiring face, then stacked pillows behind
her and tidied the bed before calling her brother in. 'Stay
here with Hilary for a few minutes, Rhys, while I get
dressed, then I'll come back and make her some
breakfast.'

'I don't want any breakfast,' said Hilary faintly.

'Of course you do,' said Rhys firmly, sitting on the edge of the bed, as his sister hurried off. 'Do as you're told, there's a good girl.'

'I'm always a good girl,' she said bitterly, and turned her head away on the pillow to hide the tears in her eyes. 'If I weren't so boringly good I wouldn't be here now like this...' She trailed away, sniffing valiantly, and with a muttered curse Rhys Probert gathered her up into his arms and held her against him, stroking her untidy hair as he pressed her head against his shoulder.

'There, there, *cariad*,' he said with surprising gentleness. 'Had a fight with Sir Galahad, I suppose. Go on. Have a good cry. Do you good.'

Hilary was mortified to find she needed no encouragement. Rhys's kindness put paid to her last shreds of control and she sobbed bitterly against his broad chest, never even noticing that it was bare, lost to everything but the ache in her ankle, which seemed all mixed up with the one in her heart.

Then suddenly she was pulled away by hard, bruising hands which tossed her aside on the bed like a bag of laundry, and she screeched in outrage as she saw Rhodri, eyes blazing, land a very punishing fist right on the point of Rhys Probert's unsuspecting jaw. Rhys went sprawling on the floor, and Rhodri stood over him, breathing hard, his fists clenched.

'What do you think you're *doing*?' shrieked Hilary in outrage, but he ignored her.

'Up on your feet!' he barked to the unfortunate Rhys, and, nothing loath, the other man jumped up, glaring at his attacker before rushing at him like a bull. The two men closed together like a pair of boys in a school playground, scuffling about ignominiously. Now that he was more prepared Rhys Probert made up for lack of height by his superior strength as the two men grappled with each other in front of Hilary's incensed eyes. A bedside lamp went crashing to the ground and she could stand no more, afraid her flat would be in ruins any minute at the present rate.

She slid out of bed and stood awkwardly on one foot, hanging on to the brass bedhead as she screamed at the men to stop. They took no notice whatsoever, and with a moan of despair Hilary began to shuffle towards the tennis racquet she could see against the wall on the far side of the room. Avoiding the combatants with difficulty, she managed to reach it, seized it in both hands and brought it crashing down on the nearest available head, which proved to be Rhodri's. He gave a violent curse and turned, clutching the back of his head just in time to see his assailant crumple in a heap on the floor.

Rhys swore and made for her, but Rhodri flung him aside, and bent, wincing, to pick her up, then halted as he saw her bandaged ankle, and sank down on his knees beside her.

'Sweetheart,' he said urgently, 'what happened?'

'She fell down that bloody staircase, you fool,' snapped Rhys, helping Rhodri lay Hilary on the bed again. He stood back, rubbing his bruised jaw as he glared at the other man. 'If you'd stopped to ask questions first you'd have known straight away, instead of trying to beat the living daylights out of me.'

Hilary lay like a log, watching dully as Rhodri looked down at her then up at Rhys, a dark flush creeping along his cheekbones as he realised things were not precisely as he'd imagined when he burst through Hilary's half-open front door.

'I apologise,' he said stiffly, but after a while a sheepish smile twitched at the corners of his mouth and he waved a hand at Rhys. 'But put yourself in my place. If you found the girl you love in a nightgown, held in the arms of a man wearing only a pair of pyjama trousers, how would you react?'

Rhys stared at him in silence for a moment, then reluctantly he began to smile, wincing as the movement hurt his jaw. He nodded. 'Like you, I suppose. But you don't know the morning we've had. Catrin and I heard a hell of a clatter as Hilary tumbled down her stairs, then half the neighbours ran out, the doctor's been——'

'Strewth!' Rhodri sat on the edge of the bed and took Hilary's lax hand in his urgently. 'Did you break anything, darling? Should you have an X-ray on that foot? Are you sure you're all right?'

Hilary glared at him. 'Go away!'

Rhodri looked as though she'd hit him again, and rubbed the back of his head. 'Not until we've had a talk,' he said heavily.

'Oh, but I didn't think mere *talk* was enough any more!' She saw Rhys shift uneasily but felt no embarrassment. In fact, she realised, apart from the dull throb in her ankle she didn't seem to be feeling anything at all. She was quite numb.

Rhodri breathed in deeply. 'You misunderstood me last night, Hilary.'

'Look,' said Rhys awkwardly. 'I'll go now——'

'No,' said Hilary. 'Stay.'

The two men exchanged looks, and Rhys smiled rather ruefully at the stormy-looking invalid. 'I really think I should get dressed, love. Penafon can only take so much in one day, you know.'

'Oh dear, you're right!' Hilary sighed. 'Of course you must go, Rhys. And thank you for picking up the pieces. I'm sorry I was such a nuisance.'

'Any time,' he assured her, and grinned. 'If you need me, thump on the floor with your tennis racquet.'

Rhodri gave him a very straight look. 'She won't need you.'

Rhys looked from Hilary's colourless, closed face to the good-looking face of the man beside her. 'No,' he agreed. 'I don't think she will. Otherwise I wouldn't leave you with her. I'd better get back to Catrin and warn her to leave you both in peace. If you need anything, just shout.'

Rhodri stood up and held out his hand. 'I repeat my apology. I took you by surprise, Probert. I know very well my fist wouldn't have had the same success if you'd seen it coming.'

Rhys looked at the proffered hand then grinned, and shook it. 'No harm done. At least,' he added with sudden meaning. 'Not to me. Take care of her.' He bent and touched Hilary's hair. 'Take it easy, *cariad*.'

She managed a smile. 'I will. Thank you again.'

When the outer door had closed on the muscular, scantily clad figure of Rhys Probert there was silence in the room for a while. Hilary pulled the quilt over her and lay with her head turned away from the man watching her so closely.

'Why did you run away, Hilary?' asked Rhodri, as the silence grew unbearable.

'You want the truth?' she said dully, turning towards him.

'Not really, by the look on your face. But tell me just the same.'

'All right. It's simple. I felt such a fool I couldn't stay. I thought you were going to propose, you see. Marriage, I mean.' Hilary's eyes were calm as they rested on his tense face. 'So I hopped it as soon as it was light.'

'I see.' Rhodri's eyes were lightless, like discs of opaque glass. 'That must have been about the time I fell into the one doze I managed all night. I got up about six and tiptoed around trying not to wake you. About seven I decided I couldn't stand to wait any more and took a cup of tea up to your room, only to find the bird had flown. So I rang Mrs Bray to ask her to come in to wait for Candida and Jack, and took off after you.' He got up and went over to the window. 'I went via Nell's place, but your car wasn't parked outside so I came straight here.'

'You made good time.'

'I was in a hurry.'

There was another awkward silence, then Rhodri turned to look down at her. Hilary gazed back without speaking, and he moved back again involuntarily.

'I love you very much, you know,' he said, so quietly she wondered if she'd heard him correctly. He smiled a little. 'I waited patiently for the three months. Did as you asked, courted you, to use an old-fashioned phrase. And in that time I decided our age difference could go to hell. If you had more growing up to do, I saw no reason why you couldn't do it just as well married to me as on your own here in Penafon.'

Hilary's heart stopped, then started again, with a thump. 'But you said you wanted to be my first *lover*——' she began, hoisting herself up against the pillows.

'I know. I do.' A light began to flicker behind the opaque glass. 'Is that so strange?'

'How about the others?' she demanded.

His smile died. 'What others?' he said harshly.

'The word "first" implied—to me at least—that you expected there to be others after you,' she said flatly, and recoiled at the sudden icy look which speared her to the bed.

'We do have a communication problem, don't we?' he said, in a tone which made her toes curl under the quilt. 'In words of one syllable, Hilary Mason, what I meant was that I want to be not only your first but your last lover, your husband, the father of your children, and, what's more, I am not in love with some other woman and I do not look on you in the light of a consolation prize, but as the greatest prize a man could ever wish for. Once I rid you of this habit of lashing out with the nearest blunt instrument on all possible occasions,' he added, rubbing the place where she'd hit him. 'I'd have told you all this last night, if you hadn't scuttled off to bed like a frightened rabbit.'

Hilary stared at him open-mouthed.

'Well?' he demanded, sitting down on the bed. 'Haven't you anything to say?'

She shook her head, the colour suddenly flooding into her cheeks, and he shrugged.

'Very well then.'

And to Hilary's consternation Rhodri Lloyd-Ellis kicked off his shoes, stripped off his clothes, and slid into bed beside her.

'What do you think you're doing?' she gasped in alarm.

'I'm dog-tired. So, by the look of it, are you. So let's go to sleep. We can go on arguing when we wake up.' And he turned her away from him, fitted himself against her with an arm around her waist, and settled himself comfortably. 'If nothing else,' he muttered into her curls, 'I'll be able to say I've slept with you once, at least.'

Hilary gave an involuntary little giggle, and he kissed her ear, then yawned, stretched a little and gave a great sigh of contentment. She lay very quietly, telling herself that this was not a good idea. But after a while it was useless to pretend it wasn't a very good idea. Both of them had passed an unhappy, sleepless night. On top of that they had both, in rather different ways, suffered trauma due to her fall. And she was very tired, she conceded, and her ankle seemed to have stopped throbbing, and she wriggled closer. Rhodri gave a little grunt of satisfaction and Hilary smiled, then yawned, then slept.

She woke to the smell of frying bacon, and her stomach rumbled as she struggled to sit up in a bed she now occupied alone. A rather musical baritone was singing 'Oh, what a beautiful mo-o-orning', in her kitchen, and Hilary smiled radiantly and hugged her arms round herself, her eyes widening as she caught sight of her watch. Far from being morning, it was almost evening.

Rhodri appeared in the doorway, smiling at her in a way which made her heart turn over. His hair was wet from a shower, and, apart from a layer of dark blond stubble, he looked wonderful.

'Come on, sleepyhead,' he said matter-of-factly. 'I've run a bath for you, so up you come.' He hoisted her in his arms and carried her the short distance to the bathroom, brushing aside her protests that she could walk unaided. Minutes later Hilary lay in blissful hot water, her ankle so much better she wondered if happiness was a cure for sprains.

'Don't be long,' yelled Rhodri. 'This is almost ready.'

'This' smelled so delicious Hilary soaped herself in a hurry, and sat on the cork bathroom stool to dry before wrapping round her the pink towelling robe which usually hung behind the door.

As she emerged, Rhodri scooped her up again and carried her into the sitting-room, depositing her carefully on the sofa before going off to fetch a tray which held plates of bacon and eggs.

'You know one of us is just going to have to learn to cook properly,' he said, as he began on his own share with enthusiasm. 'But by the time I woke up the little shop on the corner of the square was the only one open, and this was the best it could offer. Keep that foot up,' he added severely.

'It's much better now, and this is quite delicious.' Hilary grinned at him. 'I was starving.' She looked at him guiltily as something struck her. 'Oh, dear— Candida!'

'I rang her from the call-box at the end of the street,' said Rhodri indistinctly, and finished what he was eating before explaining that he'd made all the necessary explanations.

'What did you say?' asked Hilary curiously.

'The truth. The misunderstanding, the chase up here, your fall, and what I intend to do next.'

'I think I'm entitled to hear the last bit, too!'

'I said I was going to feed you, then put you back to bed,' he said simply, and took her plate. 'Have you finished?'

'Yes. Thank you, it was lovely.' Hilary eyed him challengingly. 'What did she say to that?'

'Your sister's a very practical girl. She told me the best way to keep you off your foot was to stay in bed with you.'

Hilary giggled.

'I won't even transmit Jack's message,' went on Rhodri, 'except to say that his therapy for a sprained ankle is not one generally prescribed by the medical profession.' He leered at her suggestively, and went away to wash up.

When he returned he stood looking down at Hilary, then bent to pick her up again and stood still, looking into her eyes now they were level with his own.

'Well?' he said, and she flushed and buried her face against his shoulder. 'May I take that as a general agreement with your sister?' he whispered in her ear, and Hilary nodded, bumping her forehead against his collarbone.

Rhodri walked with her into the bedroom, his cheek against her hair, and laid her gently on the bed. Hilary looked up at him trustingly, and smiled as she undid the tie of her dressing-gown. He knelt beside her, sliding it from her shoulders, his mouth on hers. Hilary trembled, and he tensed and made to move away, but she held him fast, her arms locked about his neck. As their lips opened and clung, her hands loosened and slid to unbutton his shirt, and Rhodri stood up and took off his clothes with flattering haste, coming down beside her at last to take her in his arms and hold her cruelly close.

'Now,' he breathed, 'you can't run away this time because you can't walk.'

'I don't want to run anywhere,' she said, glorying in the tautness of his body as she smoothed her hands over his shoulders.

'And you'll make an honest man of me afterwards?' he said, raising his head to look down at her.

'Yes,' she whispered, and trembled at the light in his eyes.

'You'll marry me?'

'Yes.'

He said no more, his mouth too occupied with wooing every part of her body into delighted, quivering response to caresses she gloried in and returned, making him gasp as he tried to lie still beneath the hands and lips that encroached delicately over his broad chest. His eyes opened wide as Hilary took courage and ventured a caress that changed the course of their lovemaking abruptly.

Suddenly the playing was over and Rhodri slid her willing body beneath his and held her close, his eyes glittering with a question she answered by arching her hips up to his in an invitation he responded to with such a blazing look of joy that she barely registered the pang of pain which seemed such a trifling price to pay for the sublime experience which followed it.

'Now you'll have to marry me,' he said drowsily a long time afterwards.

'Yes,' she agreed.

He raised his head to look at her. 'You agree for once?' he said with mock-severity.

Hilary stretched luxuriously, loving the feel of his body against hers. 'Yes. As I'm sure I'll never find anyone as skilled as you in this particular field, Mr Lloyd-Ellis, I think it's the only sensible thing to do.'

'You mean,' said Rhodri dramatically, 'that you only want me for my body?'

'Oh, no,' she said, shocked. 'I like your car, too!'

'I'll punish you for that,' he said darkly, but the form of punishment proved so pleasurable it was some time before he said anything again.

'I meant,' he said, returning to his original statement, 'that you'll have no alternative to marry me because all of Penafon will have heard by now that you and I are spending the night together.'

'They don't know that you're making love to me.'

'Is it likely that I'd stay the night and *not* make love to you, child?'

'I'm not a child.'

'No,' he agreed huskily, and smiled at her. 'You're not.'

Hilary spent a blissful interval convincing him of the fact. 'Do you think some library in Oxford would employ me?' she asked dreamily, after a while.

'Try some of them and see.'

'You mean you don't dislike the thought of having a working wife?'

'No. As long as she's nice and lively when I get home at night.'

'Well, since I'm so young, as you keep telling me, I'll probably manage that without too much trouble!' Hilary balanced herself on one elbow, looking down into Rhodri's face. 'You're a beautiful man, you know.' To her surprise he flushed.

'Rot,' he said, and pulled her down to him. 'You're the beautiful one.'

Hilary peered down into his eyes. 'You mean that,' she said in wonder. 'You must love me!'

'I rather thought I'd been making that fact very clear. Shall I prove it to you again?'

'Yes, please!'

Rhodri pulled her down to him, then rolled over so that he held her captive, but Hilary put up a hand to his face, curious to know something before he made her lose her wits again.

'Rhodri, you never told me what Jack suggested as a cure for my ankle.'

Rhodri smiled at her in a way that brought the quick colour to her face. 'How *is* the ankle?'

'It's much better, now I come to think of it,' said Hilary in surprise, then eyed Rhodri suspiciously as he roared with laughter. 'What's so funny?'

'Jack's ribald advice on treatment was obviously sound, then, wasn't it?'

Hilary laughed up into the dancing grey eyes. 'You mean you've already administered the prescribed remedy!'

'I certainly have. How does the patient feel?'

'Quite wonderful,' she sighed, then stretched, eyeing him from under her lashes. 'I can foresee one problem, though...'

'What is it?'

'Will you mind awfully if the patient becomes hopelessly addicted to the treatment?'

'Not in the least,' said her self-appointed physician, hugging her. 'Because as far as you're concerned, it happens to be an addiction I wholeheartedly share!'

HARLEQUIN
American Romance®

November brings you...

SENTIMENTAL JOURNEY

BARBARA BRETTON

Jitterbugging at the Stage Door Canteen, singing along with the Andrews Sisters, planting your Victory Garden—this was life on the home front during World War II.

Barbara Bretton captures all the glorious memories of America in the 1940's in SENTIMENTAL JOURNEY—a nostalgic Century of American Romance book and a Harlequin Award of Excellence title.

Available wherever Harlequin® books are sold.